ALLMEN

AND THE

PINK
DIAMOND

MARTIN SUTER

Translated by Steph Morris

NEW VESSEL PRESS
NEW YORK

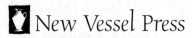
New Vessel Press

www.newvesselpress.com

First published in German in 2011 as *Allmen und der rosa Diamant*
Copyright © 2011 Diogenes Verlag AG Zürich
Translation Copyright © 2019 Stephen Morris

Library of Congress Cataloging-in-Publication Data
Suter, Martin
[Allmen und der rosa Diamant. English]
Allmen and the Pink Diamond/ Martin Suter; translation by Steph Morris.
p. cm.
ISBN 978-1-939931-63-4
Library of Congress Control Number 2018961675
I. Switzerland — Fiction

For Toni

ALLMEN

AND THE

PINK DIAMOND

PART 1

1

Allmen was nervous. The receptionist would announce Montgomery's arrival at any moment.

He was sitting behind a mahogany desk in an office at Grant Associates in Knightsbridge. Through the window, flanked by heavy curtains, he could see Hyde Park and the cars on South Carriage Drive.

It was thanks to the care he took in maintaining his network from earlier, better days that he'd been able to use this office for the meeting. This time it was an old classmate from Charterhouse who had come to the rescue, Tommy Grant, a good-natured, somewhat ponderous fellow. As family tradition dictated, he had become a lawyer, and was now senior partner of Grant Associates, a prestigious law firm in its fourth generation.

Tommy had been delighted to receive Allmen's call, had invited him to dinner with his boring wife and his two bored, teenage sons, and was now happy to lend him this office for a day. Or two, or three. Since his father had retired from active participation in the firm, the room was only used a couple of times a year.

And so he was able to receive Montgomery in the imposing premises of this traditional firm, an invaluable boost to Allmen's mission to propel Allmen International Inquiries to its long-sought international breakthrough.

In the two years since its founding, its field of operations had been limited largely to Switzerland. And to rather small-scale cases, none of them approaching the sums involved in the spectacular recovery of the dragonfly bowls, mainly involving pictures and objets d'art in the five-figure range, from clients in the art and antiques sector.

Carlos had created the website allmen-international. com on his secondhand computer. Allmen had written the copy and determined the look. The homepage had a flannel-gray background. Right at the top of the screen, spaced evenly across the width, were the names of the five cities, in an elegantly proportioned, classic silver Antiqua: New York, Zurich, Paris, London, Moscow. Beneath them, a little larger, "Allmen International Inquiries," followed by the slogan Allmen was rather proud of: "The art of tracing art," solely in English, as it didn't translate so elegantly into German.

This somewhat grandiloquent Internet presence couldn't disguise for more than a glance that Allmen International Inquiries hadn't yet managed to distinguish itself from a shady, backroom detective agency.

The agency's income came largely from the hourly rates they charged their clients, with occasional commissions on successful finds, and a small percentage of the recovered items' value, correspondingly modest.

For Carlos this income nevertheless allowed him to reduce

his day job as gardener and caretaker for the trust company that had bought Allmen's Villa Schwarzacker to a part-time position. But in terms of Allmen's lifestyle it was peanuts. He was frequently forced to sell off items from his collection of fine objects. And soon he would have to return to cashing in items he had acquired in other ways. Whatever, wherever.

That was why everything had to be in place for this meeting with Montgomery.

"Will you see Mr. Montgomery, sir?"

Allmen jumped. The voice came from the old-fashioned intercom, set at a high volume for Mr. Grant senior, who was hard of hearing. He pressed the worn talk button and had him sent in.

Montgomery was a shade younger than Allmen, late thirties perhaps. He wore a well-cut business suit and had a suntan, his cropped hair prematurely gray. He entered the room confidently, without looking around, as if he were used to such interiors.

Allmen stood up as he entered and walked toward him. As they greeted, he registered that his guest did not speak the kind of upper-class English his appearance might have suggested.

He offered him an armchair, part of the matching heavy leather furniture, and sat opposite.

"Tea?"

Montgomery declined. He placed an angular, battered executive case on the table in front of him, opened both locks, and extracted a thin folder. Then he looked Allmen in the eyes.

Montgomery's eyes were a watery blue. In the whites around the iris were a few black specks of pigment, which made it hard for Allmen to hold his gaze.

"How long do we have?" was Montgomery's first question.

"As long as you need."

"Not long then."

Allmen responded in the same businesslike tone. "That suits me too."

Montgomery got straight to the point. "I'm sure I don't need to repeat that everything I tell you today is strictly confidential."

"Par for the course," Allmen said.

Montgomery leaned back in the armchair. "A pink diamond. Do you know what I'm talking about?"

Allmen, an avid reader, had followed the recent story in the papers about the auction of a pink diamond at the Swiss branch of Murphy's. The stone had fetched a record price.

"Yes. One recently went to an anonymous bidder for over forty-five million Swiss francs."

"Thirty million pounds." Montgomery left a meaningful pause before saying, "The man is my client."

"I see. The diamond has disappeared." This sounded like an assertion, as if the information was not news to Allmen.

No comment from Montgomery. His spotted eyes maintained contact.

Allmen took a sheet of Allmen International Inquiries stationery, lying at the ready, and wrote "Meeting Montgomery," along with the date and location, just below the letterhead. Then he looked at Montgomery in anticipation.

The latter leaned forward, resting his arms on his thighs. "I'm not allowed to disclose the details. But I'll say this much: my client held a private reception in one of his villas, at a location that's irrelevant to our purposes. His wife was wearing the diamond. Next day it was no longer to be seen."

Allmen waited, poised to note something.

"I know it's not much," Montgomery said.

"And how should we …" Allmen spoke in the plural when alluding to his multinational enterprise. "How are we to find the item without a single clue?"

"We are carrying out investigations in my client's immediate surroundings ourselves. But now we have reached a point where we believe it makes sense to bring in third parties."

Allmen was still waiting for something worth noting down.

"We have identified the go-between."

"And why don't you have him arrested?"

Montgomery reached into his jacket and took out a packet of cigarettes. "Do you mind if I smoke here?"

Allmen, who tended to describe himself as a non-practicing smoker, hated it when people smoked in his personal space. But he had never answered such a question in the affirmative. He expected his smoker guests to be tactful enough not to ask. But now the question put him on the spot. Tommy Grant had specifically requested that he not smoke in the office, out of consideration for his father's asthma.

He was still wondering how to reply as Montgomery slipped the cigarettes back in his pocket, without a word. "Two reasons why we aren't having him arrested. First, my client doesn't wish to involve the authorities in the search for something he never officially owned. Second, the man has gone underground."

Allmen nodded. This explanation seemed plausible. "And when we find him? What do we do, if you don't wish to get the authorities involved?"

"When you've found him, follow him and let us know. Then we'll discuss the next stage."

Montgomery handed him the folder he had been holding in his hand the whole time. It contained a sheet of paper that looked at first glance like a resume. It bore the header "Artyom Sokolov." A photo was attached to the top right corner with a paper clip. It showed an emaciated man with thinning, combed-back hair and sunken eyes.

The information was scant: Born 1974 in Yekaterinburg, around 6'2" tall, 187 pounds, medium blond, studied electrical engineering, degree in computer science, worked as a freelance IT specialist. Last known location Switzerland, and there was an address: Gelbburgstrasse 13, Apt. 12, 8694 Schwarzegg.

Allmen looked up from the paper and met Montgomery's eyes, which must have been fixed on him as he read this brief information. "How did you hear about us?"

"I made some inquiries. Your track record impressed me. The dragonfly bowl case above all. The police search for the best part of a decade for them; your agency finds them in seconds—respect."

Allmen let the sentence echo in his head to see if it sounded ironic. He decided it didn't.

"We liked the fact that you're a small outfit—the person it's named after is still actively involved. And an international operation, which fits our needs."

Still no irony to be detected.

"But, be honest now …"

Allmen looked up from the folder, to which he had lowered his eyes in modesty during the praise.

"Are you quite sure this job isn't too big for you? Now would be the moment to tell me. Last exit."

How was someone who had lived beyond his means for most of his life supposed to weigh up whether something was too big for him? Allmen simply smiled. "Thank you for the opportunity." Then he turned to his sheet of paper and made a note in shorthand.

During his time as a drifting international student he had taken a course in the Stolze Schrey stenography system. Not because there was much likelihood he would put it to real use, but because he hoped to attract the attention of his fellow students and his father, which he succeeded in doing.

He had retained this skill. His shorthand had become increasingly individualized, becoming his personal secret code. He loved it, as he loved everything secretive.

Montgomery also seemed impressed. For the first time, when Allmen looked up, he saw that Montgomery was not looking into his eyes but down at the paper.

"What are your terms and conditions?" he wanted to know.

Although finance was fundamental to Allmen, he hated to discuss it. Carlos had prepared him a sheet with all the key points listed. Allmen didn't have it at hand, emphasizing how immaterial the subject was. He stood up, went to the desk, pretended to look for something and finally returned with two pieces of paper, both titled "Fee Agreement."

The hourly rate was between 80 and 150, depending on the expertise of the staff member and the complexity of the task. Research and investigation were more expensive than simple surveillance for instance. Alongside this came expenses and commission in the event of a successful recovery, either an additional ten percent of the total fees or, should the value of the item be higher, ten percent of that sum. Whether the fee was paid in Swiss francs, euros, dollars, or pounds depended on the country in question.

He handed this fee agreement to Montgomery, who scanned it and placed it on the club table.

"And what is your invoicing procedure?"

In this area he and Carlos had agreed on flexibility. Depending on the client's reaction, Allmen International would either invoice for the exact work done or request advance payments on account. Montgomery's reaction suggested the second model.

"We take payments on account. The account is then settled—in your favor or ours—at the end of the operation."

"And what is the down-payment sum?"

"Twenty thousand. In your case pounds."

Montgomery fished an envelope out of his executive case and pushed it across the table. "Ten okay?"

Allmen registered this without comment. He left the envelope lying nonchalantly where Montgomery had left it.

"And then there's the commission. In our case you can hardly reckon with ten percent." Montgomery unscrewed the lid of his fountain pen.

"I think in this instance we could make an exception and offer eight percent."

"Four," Montgomery decided. He crossed out the "ten" on each agreement, wrote "four," signed and dated both copies, and handed them over. Allmen signed both in turn and placed his copy next to the envelope with the money.

After they had parted company Allmen stood by the window and looked down at the street. He saw Montgomery leave the front door with his phone to his ear. Now he snapped it shut and pocketed it. Barely a minute later, a black Range Rover pulled up at the curb. On the passenger side a man got out, gave his seat to Montgomery, and closed the door. He waited till there was a gap in the traffic and the car could drive off, then took advantage of the next gap, crossing the street at speed and vanishing into the park. The man was carrying a black sports bag over one shoulder.

Allmen did three things next, which if the meeting had gone less favorably, he would have refrained from.

He walked to the Wilton Arms, his favorite Knightsbridge pub, and drank two deliciously warm, brimful, froth-free half pints of bitter.

He paid a surprise visit to his tailor on Savile Row and ordered a three-piece suit in a wonderful Donegal.

And at Claridge's he had himself upgraded from his junior suite to a proper suite.

As he got into his cab to the airport the next morning, he noticed a man. He was photographing the hotel entrance, carrying a black sports bag over his shoulder.

2

Carlos met him wearing the blue apron he wore to clean shoes. He took Allmen's case and mackintosh and followed him into the greenhouse library.

It was a summer afternoon and he had lowered the faded orange blinds to block light coming through the glazed roof; they had once been used to protect plants from direct sunlight, now books. The curtains were drawn too. The rays of sun that shot here and there through the gaps in the blackout gave the large room a theatrical air.

The piano stool was standing at the ready, surrounded by the majority of Allmen's shoes. None of them genuinely needed polishing.

Allmen sat down and placed his right foot on the black shoeshine box. Carlos began brushing. He asked no questions, simply waiting for Allmen to start talking.

"Carlos, this is Allmen International Inquiries' international breakthrough."

"*No me diga*," Carlos replied. "You don't say." He took a cloth from the box and drizzled liquid over the shoe from a small plastic bottle. He had never said what it was, and Allmen had never asked. He wouldn't have been surprised if it had simply been water.

Allmen told him about the pink diamond, worth forty-five million, and the 1.8 million commission this would mean.

Carlos listened in silence. Tapped his index finger under the tip of each foot when Allmen was to switch feet, and murmured *"por favor"* when he wanted his customer to put another pair on.

The shoes were lined up, shined to perfection, Allmen had reached the end of his report, and still Carlos had barely said a word.

"Qué pasa, Carlos? Why aren't you saying anything?" Allmen asked.

Carlos had begun piling the shoes in a clothes basket ready to sort them back into Allmen's shoe cupboard. Now he broke off from his work. "The case is too big for Allmen International, Don John. We shouldn't accept the job."

"You mean the sums of money are too big?"

"Everything about it is too big."

Allmen didn't understand exactly what Carlos meant. Perhaps he shared the feeling that had briefly overcome Allmen himself on the return flight, that he was poised to enter a world of wholly new dimensions. People who were willing and able to pay forty-five million francs for a ring were capable of anything. And people willing and able to *steal* forty-five-million-franc rings …

"Allmen International will rise to the challenge," Allmen answered.

Carlos shook his head. *"Con todo el respeto,* I think it would be shrewder for Allmen International Inquiries to turn the job down."

"Think of everything we've already invested in it. The travel costs, the hotel …"

Strictly speaking, it wasn't Allmen International that had made this investment. It was Carlos. Not for the first time since the firm's inception, he had made the agency a loan from his share of the dragonfly commission, his personal savings. According to his accounts the agency now owed him more than the start-up capital of twenty thousand francs they had contributed equally when the company was founded. In a real sense Allmen International Inquiries belonged to Carlos Santiago de Leon. But due to his status as an illegal immigrant he could only be a silent partner, so there was no record in the commercial register of his de facto expropriation of Allmen.

In mentioning the investments Allmen had touched Carlos's raw nerve. Finance was his weak point too, but in the opposite sense: whereas for Allmen everything revolved around money because of his extravagance, for Carlos it was because of his thrift.

And now Allmen topped it: "Then there's the fact that Allmen International Inquiries has already taken the down payment."

Carlos made no reply. He knew his *patrón* well enough not to suggest he return the money. He knew he could count himself lucky if there was any of it left for the housekeeping.

3

Allmen had asked Herr Arnold to leave his 1978 Cadillac Fleetwood in the garage today and chauffeur him in his everyday Mercedes diesel. It went against the grain, but it was necessary to preserve his anonymity as an investigator.

They drove through the city's urban sprawl toward Schwarzegg, a suburb close to the airport. The hazy sky was crosshatched with vapor trails. Allmen had opened the window. It smelled of tar and summer.

Gelbburgstrasse was at the edge of the city, a tract of bleak 1980s apartment blocks surrounded by monotonous expanses of grass. Mathematically aligned concrete sidewalks led past trash containers and bike racks to each building.

Allmen got out at the path leading to number fourteen. The building had recently been done up. Above the entrance, a canopy of chrome and glass had been erected to give the impression of tasteful modernity. Allmen entered the hall. It smelled of cleaning products. A man in work clothes was sitting on a machine polishing the floor—flecked yellow, reconstituted stone. He ignored Allmen.

There was no name on the letterbox for apartment 12, just the fragments of a torn-off nameplate. In the elevator, the button for the third floor was labeled "Apartments 8-12."

The doorbell to the apartment was not identified with a name either. Allmen pressed it.

To his surprise the door opened immediately. He was hit by the thick, stale air of unventilated rooms. A medium-tall blond man stood in front of him. He was wearing a shirt with the collar open and a loosened tie, along with colorful sweatpants. His feet were shoved into hotel slippers, no longer terribly white.

"Yes?" he asked, managing to say this one word with such a strong accent Allmen immediately knew he was dealing with a Hungarian.

"Sorry to disturb you. I'm looking for Mr. Solokov."

"I don't know him."

"I've been told he can be found at this address." Allmen held his notebook with the address under the man's nose.

He cast a swift look at it. "The address is correct, but not the name. People come and go. Business apartments."

"I see. Your predecessor."

The man shrugged his shoulders. "Or the one before him. Why don't you ask in the office?"

"Which office?"

"The real estate agency. They rent this place out. Wait a moment."

The man vanished from Allmen's view. He heard the plopping of tennis balls and the lethargic observations of a television commentator. In the hallway was a half-open suitcase revealing its disorganized contents.

The man returned with a diary. "Immolandia is the company's name. I thought I had a card, but I must have given it to the man before you."

"The man before?"

"You're the third person to ask about Sokolov."

He dictated the address to Allmen. Before Allmen had even had the chance to thank him, the door closed again.

4

The offices of Immolandia were in a refurbished corner shop in a suburban district of the city. In the little plate-glass window hung marketing photos of elegant apartments with models dressed as businessmen. Above them it read, "Immolandia, your specialist for temporary business apartments!"

Allmen climbed the three steps to the door and entered the offices. Two desks with computers, four matching armchairs, and on the walls, photographs of the actual properties. They were somewhat less elegant than the idealized images in the window.

It smelled of cigarettes and stale coffee on a burner, steaming away.

A woman in her late thirties was sitting behind a screen at one of the desks. As Allmen entered she looked up crossly and sized up the man disturbing her. Based on the way he was dressed she identified a potential client and smiled. She half-stood and offered him the visitor's chair in front of her desk.

Allmen introduced himself, whipped out his wallet, and gave her a business card. He'd had two versions printed. One reading "Johann Friedrich von Allmen," with "International Inquiries" below, two points smaller. Another with "Allmen International" as the main text, his full name below, discreetly, followed by the letters "CEO." In this situation he chose the latter.

Only when he had handed over the card did he sit down opposite the woman. She examined it and asked, even more impressed now, "How can I be of assistance?"

Her lips retained the traces of lipstick, mainly adhering now to the butts filling the ashtray along with a glowing cigarette. She stubbed it out. "Excuse my smoking. We don't get many walk-in customers here. Our business is mostly over the Internet."

"Feel free to smoke. It doesn't bother me," Allmen lied. Then he got to the point. "Two things. Firstly, we often need medium-term accommodations for our international team. I'd like to collect some information about your agency to pass along to our human resources department."

The woman got up, opened a filing cabinet, and began fishing out brochures, folders, leaflets, and a range of promotional material. She was a little overweight, which didn't seem to bother her. When she reached for the top drawer, her spare tire was exposed; when she bent down for the lowest, the lace trimmings of her panties.

She placed the information in a large envelope, passed it to him, and sat back down. "And the second thing?"

"Just a query. A business associate gave me this address, but when I tried to call on him, he had moved out already. I wanted to ask if you had his new address." He passed her a memo with Solokov's name and the Gelbburgstrasse address.

"Does he owe you money too?"

Allmen wasn't surprised. "No, why?"

"You aren't the first person to ask about Mr. Solokov."

"Who else then?"

"First there was an English man. Then an American. I couldn't help either of them. Mr. Solokov didn't leave a forwarding address."

"What shall I do now?" Allmen's helplessness looked so genuine the woman took pity on him.

"Most of our tenants return to their home countries. Then it's tricky. But if not, try the registration office. They can tell you where someone has moved to or from. You just have to bring proof of interest."

"What would that be?"

"A contract, a court ruling, a loss certificate from the debt enforcement office, or some kind of proof that he owes you money."

"He doesn't owe me money."

"Sometimes a credible explanation for why you need to find him is enough. Those officials aren't quite so inflexible these days."

"Good idea," he said. "Thanks for the tip." He stood up, said goodbye, and started to leave.

"What about the information?" The woman pointed to the envelope he had left lying on the desk.

He came back and took it. "Nearly forgot the most important thing," he said, shaking his head.

"Depending on the volume of bookings," she called after him, "we can offer highly competitive rates."

5

It was such a hot day Carlos had made ceviche: raw seafood marinated in lime juice, with chili, coriander, ginger, and onions. He served it outside at the garden table, under the plum tree, which never bore fruit because it got too little sun.

Allmen had declared the meal a "business lunch" to persuade Carlos to sit at the table with him. Otherwise he would insist on serving Allmen his meals in a white waiter's jacket, eating his own in the kitchen.

Over in the villa it was lunch break. A few employees of the trust company were making the most of the summer day and eating their sandwiches on the benches the management had placed around the grounds. In sight, but not in earshot.

"Englishmen and gringos," Carlos repeated thoughtfully.

"Do you think Montgomery hedged his bets and contracted other agencies too?" Allmen sounded rather worried.

"For a forty-five million item, Don John, it wouldn't surprise me."

"He should have informed me then, don't you think?"

Carlos reflected. "Perhaps he knows nothing about it.

Perhaps his client has employed other people directly." He stood up, took the bottle of Aigle from the ice bucket, wiped it dry with the napkin, and refilled Allmen's glass in the correct posture of a waiter. Then he sat down as a guest again.

Allmen thanked him and took a sip of wine. "Or perhaps he shares your view that the matter is too large for Allmen International."

There was silence for a while as they ate marinated squid, shrimp, and fish from the tall coupe glasses.

"Do you have an idea, Carlos?"

"*Una sugerencia, nada más*," Carlos replied modestly. Just a thought …

Allmen had learned to take such suggestions seriously. "In the brochure for the apartment building in Gelbburgstrasse it lists the restaurants, bars, shops, laundromats, and sports facilities in the area."

Allmen nodded. He had also noticed this.

"And a nightclub."

"Lonely Nights," Allmen affirmed. "And?"

"*Una sugerencia, nada más*," Carlos repeated.

"You mean, it's an apartment building full of single men. And single men tend to visit nightclubs."

"Maybe someone there knows him."

"Maybe." Allmen decided to take a rather longer siesta today. It could be a late night.

6

Lonely Nights was situated in the basement of the budget Intotel, "ten minutes on foot from Gelbburgstrasse," as it said in the real estate brochure. Allmen stood in front of the hideous complex, then descended the stairs; above them, in pink neon, the words "Lonely Nights."

A display case was mounted on the wall by the door, with three or four photos of Asian girls wearing nothing but tiny black "censored" strips.

The door was locked. Next to it, under a brass doorbell, it said, "Please Ring."

Allmen did so, and the door opened in a second. A bearded man in a black suit looked him briefly up and down and let him in. Without a word.

The brightest point was a small stage lit by a single spotlight. In the circle it threw, one of the Asian girls pictured in the vitrine was dancing to loud techno music. The rest of the club was submerged in gloom. Allmen's eyes had to adjust to the light before he could find his way around.

A handful of tables were grouped in front of the stage, barely lit. Alongside them a bar ran the entire length of the room. Artistic nudes hung on the walls, each illuminated by a dim spotlight.

Allmen sat at the bar and ordered a vodka Perrier with ice and lemon.

"Will a different brand of water do?" the bartender said, a motherly blond wearing a lot of makeup and glitter.

Not really. But Allmen wanted to get on her good side, and said, "Of course. And for you?"

Now she smiled, showing a set of very regular, very white teeth. "The same. But without the water, ice, and lemon."

Farther down the bar, two men were deep in conversation, backs to the stage. Between them and Allmen, one man was sitting alone. His elbows rested on the bar behind him as he gobbled up the dancer with his eyeballs. Only two of the tables were occupied. At one a man was sitting with a dancing girl. At another were three girls, who looked over to Allmen.

He took his drink, raised the glass to the bartender, and turned to watch the dancer.

The show consisted of an unerotic aerobics act, which did nothing for him. Nevertheless, he watched out of polite interest, as he did whenever someone performed for him. Even during the cabin crew's security demonstration before takeoff, which he had seen a thousand times, he would never read the paper or look out the window. It was a matter of respect, in Allmen's view. If someone made the effort to present something for him, they had the right to his attention.

The music stopped abruptly, and the naked dancer

bowed, very low. With her back to the meager audience. All-men was the only one to applaud.

He turned back to his drink. The matron behind the bar smiled at him and emptied her glass.

"Another?" Allmen asked.

She poured herself one and came over to him. "What brings you to this neck of the woods? Business?"

"Sure. But I also wanted to visit a friend who lives round here. Except now he's moved and I don't know where."

"This close to the airport people don't really settle. If they aren't simply passing through anyway, the noise drives them away." She looked past him into the club. "Would you like some company?"

"I have company."

She glanced past him again with a very slight shake of her head.

"His name is Sokolov. Artyom Sokolov."

"The guests here don't tend to have names. What does he look like then?"

Allmen hesitated. Then he took Sokolov's photo out of his wallet and passed it to her. She scrutinized Allmen. "You're not a cop; you're too well dressed."

She went toward the cash register, put on a pair of glasses and switched on a little lamp.

One of the Asian girls took advantage of the brief moment Allmen was alone and sat on the barstool next to him. He recognized her as the stripper he had just watched.

"You all on your own?" she asked.

The bartender returned and made a casual gesture to

the dancing girl, indicating she should disappear.

"It's okay," Allmen said to the barwoman. And to the stripper he said, "What are you drinking?"

"Piccolo," she smiled.

Allmen ordered a bottle of Dom Pérignon, only to discover that in Lonely Nights the top of the range was Veuve Clicquot. At 270 Swiss francs.

The stripper was delighted, however. She fell around Allmen's neck and confided her name was Rosy. "Like a rose. But I don't have thorns," she added.

The bartender, "Gerta" Rosy called her, brought the champagne, the ice bucket, and two glasses. Allmen asked for a third. Not because he planned to switch to champagne. He just knew that in establishments like this it was about emptying the bottle, not drinking it.

But in Lonely Nights in Schwarzegg the rules were different. Veuve Clicquot was ordered so rarely it was gladly drunk.

And so Gerta filled three glasses and raised hers to the others'. Then she gave him his photo back. "He might have come here once or twice."

Rosy took the picture off her. "Looks like the Russian."

"Lots of Russians come here," Gerta interjected.

"The one with the nine bottles."

Gerta studied the picture again carefully and gave it back to Allmen. "Maybe."

"Definitely. I saw him closer up than you," Rosy said pointedly.

"If that's him," the bartender explained to Allmen,

"he once forked out for nine bottles of champagne. Not Veuve Clicquot, just house champagne, but still. Birthday or something."

"Not his birthday," Rosy corrected her, "an amazing business deal. He said he was celebrating an amazing deal."

"When was that?"

The women looked at each other, unsure. "Roughly a month ago," Gerta suggested. Rosy agreed.

Allmen was disappointed. That was too far back. Sokolov couldn't have been celebrating the pink diamond with those nine bottles of champagne.

"One minute," Gerta murmured, and went off. Allmen saw her exchange a few words with the two men at the other end of the bar. One of them accompanied her back.

Gerta introduced the man as Ted. He was a short, scruffy Irishman who looked like a retired jockey.

"Can you show Ted the photo?" the bartender asked him.

The Irishman examined it and nodded. "Looks like Arti. A bit younger, but it's Arti. What do you want from him?"

"I was in the area and wanted to visit him, but he's left his apartment without leaving a forwarding address."

Ted nodded. "There one minute, gone the next."

Allmen shook his head and laughed. "Typical Arti. Never still for long. You don't have any idea …?"

Ted shook his head as well. "And if I did, I wouldn't tell you. When a man leaves no address behind, it's for a reason."

Allmen agreed wholeheartedly with him. He wouldn't expect anything else from a friend. "But perhaps his employer could help me," he suggested.

Ted shrugged his shoulders. "Arti was freelance. His own boss. He did programming for all kinds of people. You know Arti, nothing meant more to him than his freedom."

Allmen nodded in agreement. "And he probably never said who he was working freelance for."

Ted laughed. "Not Arti. The soul of discretion."

Ted was so taken with Allmen he assured him again and again he would help if he could. By the time Allmen had ordered a third bottle he said if he knew where Sokolov lived or who he was working for, he would happily tell him.

"I'd tell you," he added, "but not the other two."

"Which other two?" Allmen asked.

"The ones who came asking about Arti a few days ago. Not them."

"English guys? Americans?"

"Both."

It was nearly 2:00 a.m. before Allmen left Lonely Nights. He gave Rosy-but-I-don't-have-thorns a kiss on the hand in farewell. And a generous tip since, for reasons he would explain next time, right now he couldn't accept her suggestion to take a room in the Intotel.

7

When Carlos brought Allmen his early morning tea he normally said no more than "*Muy buenos días,* Don John." He brought it at five to seven each day, not a good time for a conversation with Allmen.

On this of all mornings, when Allmen's head was heavier than ever, his tongue more parched, Carlos decided to make an exception. To his "*Muy buenos días,* Don John," he added a "*Cómo amenció usted?*" A rather formal way of asking after someone's health in the morning.

At this time, and in this state, it was a question to which Allmen had no specific answer beyond "*Muy bien, gracias.*"

Carlos placed the cup on the bedside table and waited.

"I'll report back later, when you have more time."

Carlos started work at seven. Allmen could go back to sleep for a while.

But Carlos said, "I've got time. It's only a quarter to." He was so curious to know the results of Allmen's nocturnal researches, he had taken the liberty of waking his *patrón* ten minutes early.

He was all the more disappointed once Allmen had finished his short report.

"*Lo siento*, that's all," Allmen apologized.

"*No tengo pena,*" Carlos assured him. "If you could get the receipts ready, so I can calculate the expenses."

Then he wished him a good day and asked to be excused. "*Con permiso.*"

Expenses were an ongoing issue. It was against Allmen's nature to collect receipts. That was for cheapskates. A man of the world was not concerned with where his money had gone.

He sat up, stuffed a pillow behind his back and sipped the tea, lukewarm now.

No one vanished without a trace. But sometimes the trace vanished. Like the end of a length of wool, lost in the ball. They just had to find it before someone else did.

8

It was Carlos who picked up the thread again.

"Gelbburgstrasse," he said, with that persistence bordering at times on irritating obstinacy. "Gelbburgstrasse is our best bet."

Allmen made a start on identifying who Sokolov's clients might have been—for which he was entirely reliant on Carlos's Internet-research skills—while Carlos gave some thought to the apartment block. In the brochure he finally found his inspiration: "Cleaning service, once a week, including trash disposal."

That was it. They had to continue their investigation one social stratum lower. Allmen was the wrong man for that job. But Carlos was certainly dependent on him during the preparatory stages. He went to the library, where Allmen liked to read for an hour after his siesta, and outlined his plan.

Allmen reached for the telephone and called Immolandia. The woman who had helped him the day before answered. She sounded pleased to hear from him again so soon.

Herr von Allmen had a purely technical question. "I see in your brochure that the apartments are cleaned once a week. Which day is that normally? Our teams work mainly from home and frequently participate in international video conferences. It would be unfortunate if they were disturbed by the cleaning staff."

Carlos had come up with this story. The woman from Immolandia didn't question its plausibility for a second and asked Allmen to wait a second.

After some time she returned with the information that it depended on the floor in question. "First and second floors Tuesdays, third and fourth Wednesdays."

"Mornings or afternoons?"

She asked Allmen to wait again. He heard her talking on the other line. "Mornings," was the result of her inquiries.

Allmen thanked her, and promised to pass the information to the relevant department, who would be in touch directly.

Tomorrow was Wednesday.

9

Overnight the temperature dropped, and it rained so hard Carlos had to get up several times to empty the pots and bowls under the leaks in the library's glass roof.

Now, first thing in the morning, it had started raining again, and Carlos, who did his part-time hours either in the morning or afternoon, depending on the weather and the tasks in question, had taken this morning off.

On the way from Schwarzegg station to Gelbburgstrasse he had to open his umbrella. In the other hand he held the suit bag with the suit in it. When it got too heavy, he swapped it with the umbrella. He had to switch increasingly often.

Outside the house was a station wagon with a taxi sign. The driver was helping his passenger stash a large amount of luggage into the trunk. Carlos took the lift to the third floor.

The door to apartment 12 was open. In the hallway were a few bags of trash and a suitcase. "Hello?" Carlos called. No answer.

"Who are you looking for?" a voice asked behind him. It was the man he had just seen loading the taxi.

"Are you Mr. Sokolov?"

"He hasn't lived here for a long time." The man went in and took the luggage. "And neither do I anymore."

"Do you know his new address?" Carlos thought he might as well give it a shot.

"No, but I'm starting to be interested." He shut the door and left, without a parting word.

Carlos walked from one door to the next. Nowhere was a cleaning crew to be seen. He climbed a floor higher. There, outside apartment 15, was a cleaning trolley. The door was half open. A vacuum wailed from inside.

"Hello?" Carlos shouted. "*Con permiso?*"

The vacuum was silenced. A dumpy, gray-haired woman came to the door. "*Sí?*"

Carlos was in luck. The woman was from Ecuador. That would make the conversation easier.

"I'm looking for Mr. Sokolov, apartment 12."

"He doesn't live here anymore."

"I know. I just met the next guy. He doesn't live here anymore either."

"No one stays here long."

"How can I find out his new address?"

The woman shrugged her shoulders. "You aren't the only one who wants to know that."

Carlos sighed theatrically and lifted the suit bag up indignantly. "And what am I to do with this now?"

"Are you from the dry cleaners?"

"Dry cleaners? Tailor! This is a tailored suit!" Carlos undid the zipper. One of Allmen's many suits was revealed.

Made of a very pale cashmere, in a shade his *patrón* had later regretted, the suit had never been worn.

"Have a feel. Worth over six thousand!"

The woman slipped one of her rubber gloves off and felt the fabric, full of awe. "*Una maravilla!*" she exclaimed.

"Who's going to pay me now?" Carlos seemed on the brink of tears.

The woman softened. "Have you got a pen?"

Carlos closed the zipper on the suit bag, placed it cautiously on the ground and took a notepad and ballpoint out of his breast pocket.

"Maria Moreno," the woman said. "From Colombia. She used to work here too. She said Sokolov had offered her a job as housekeeper."

"And? Did she take it?"

"Don't know. At any rate she left at the same time he left. Maria Moreno."

"Got it. And?"

"From Colombia."

"Yes. Got it. And?"

"And nothing. Maria Moreno. I don't know any more. Maria Moreno from Colombia."

Carlos sighed. "Do you work for Immolandia or for a cleaning company?"

The woman looked suspicious. "Why?"

"They must have her address in their databank."

She looked at him as someone might look at a dimwitted child. Now Carlos got it. Maria Moreno's immigration status was like his: illegal.

He thanked the woman and said goodbye.

The train was almost empty and three teenagers were sitting on the steps to the top deck passing a joint between them. Rain flowed down the windowpanes.

Carlos put the suit bag carefully on the luggage rack, swept the commuter newspapers aside, and sat down.

He hadn't got much further than his *patrón*.

10

The Putamayo Club consisted of a sign saying "Putamayo Club" in colorful letters, framed by orchids. During the week it hung over the regulars' table at the Alte Kanonier Tavern, among the pictures of soccer players, club emblems, photos of the bar regulars, playing cards, and dish-of-the-day offers.

But every Thursday it graced the entrance to the small ballroom between the bar and the bowling alley. There, the Colombians met.

The Alte Kanonier was in an outer district of the city. Their taxi stopped at a corner building, its upper floors looking over the crisscrossing tracks of the freight depot. An illuminated sign with a logo for a long defunct brand of beer read "Alte Kanonier." There were two steps up to the entrance. Light shone through a latticed yellow pane.

The bar was quiet. A few men were playing cards at the regulars' table. At another sat an old couple, indulging in a meal out. An exhausted woman was eating with her three adolescent children. A young couple were having an awkward discussion and four young men in sweat suits were drinking beer.

Carlos went ahead, past the bar and down a corridor. Loud salsa music blasted through a door as a barmaid came toward them with a tray full of empty glasses. They entered the Putamayo Club.

The room was not as full as it sounded from outside. The Colombians were sitting at long tables watching the handful of people dancing. Conversation was only possible by shouting. If any of the guests had been doing so, now they were silenced by the arrival of this odd couple.

Allmen and Carlos sat at one of the long tables, nodded to the people already sitting, and waited till the music allowed conversation. It was a long wait.

The silence when it finished was as overwhelming as the music had been deafening. The guests sat suddenly mute in front of their drinks and smiled at each other, waiting, it seemed, for some background noise against which they could talk to each other.

The man sitting closest to them, accompanied by two middle-aged women, was also the first to pluck up the courage. "I've not seen you here before," he said to Carlos.

"It's our first time here," Carlos replied.

"No me diga!" their neighbor cried. "You don't say!"

"I'm sure it's not *your* first time," Allmen observed.

"Me?" The man revealed a gold incisor. "I co-founded the Putamayo Club. Eight years ago. My name is Alfredo, by the way."

"Then you probably know every Colombian in the city," Carlos suggested.

"There aren't many I don't know." The man basked for

a while in this fact. "Four hundred thirty-two members—we started with sixteen—in eight years!"

Now Carlos cried out *"No me diga!"* in disbelief.

Although he had lived in Carlos's company for many years, Allmen had never gotten used to the elaborate ceremony of such conversations.

He watched as the dance partners from earlier prepared to start up again, while a few of the younger club members crowded around the music system and rummaged through the CDs.

"This is just a normal club night. But you should come when we celebrate the Battle of Boyocá. Or Independence Day. Then we have to rent the barroom too. And there are still people waiting in line outside.

Allmen was starting to lose his patience. "Then perhaps you could help us," he said.

"Con mucho gusto," Alfredo said.

The music now made any further conversation impossible.

Not till the next pause could Carlos and Allmen pop their question.

"Maria Moreno?" Alfredo repeated, looking inquiringly at his two companions. They repeated the name too. "Maria Moreno?"

All three shook their heads.

At this point Allmen International Inquiries might have given up, if one of the women hadn't then ventured, "And what do you want from her?"

"Somebody I know spoke highly of her. If you see her, ask her to call me." Allmen passed her his card. The man took it out of her hand, examined it, and put it in his pocket.

They were still engaged in the elaborate farewell ceremony when the music excused them from it.

11

At Viennois the usual post-10:00 a.m. guests were in attendance. Allmen was sitting at his regular table, between the retired literary critic, who shared croissants dipped in a latte with his heavy-breathing Pekingese, and the model, no longer in her prime either and juggling two cell phones. One for incessant chatter, another in case of calls from her agent.

He drank his coffee as always, ate a croissant, and read a story. Today it was Anton Chekhov, "Anna on the Neck."

The two ancient ladies who arrived and departed in separate taxis were absorbed in their lethargic conversation, revolving, it appeared, around the appearance of the passersby they were watching from their window seats. And as usual, the man who occupied all the chairs at his table with his coat, hat, briefcase, and shopping bags, was furtively clipping articles from the café's newspapers with his pocketknife scissors. At the table where the three shop owners met, the fourth chair was still kept free—in memory of the antiques dealer Tanner, who had lost his life thanks to the dragonfly bowls.

There were few places where Allmen felt so at home as

this old-fashioned café. He had come here even as a student, when he couldn't stand it any longer on his father's farm. For him, the clinking cups, the snorting Lavazza espresso machine, and the muffled, relaxed voices were more homey sounds than the snorting and stamping of the cows in the barn at his parents' house.

Allmen put his book on the table, took a sip of coffee, and looked around. The doctor's receptionist returned with a tray of dirty cups and drank an espresso at the counter while she waited for a new round of orders to be filled. Even the two city bureaucrats were there, bickering as always for the privilege of paying the coffee-and-croissants bill.

A cellphone played a silly tune. Only when he felt it vibrating in his jacket did Allmen realize it was his. He was constantly asking Carlos to change the ringtone. But all of them were embarrassing.

He answered. A woman asked, in Spanish, "Are you Señor Allmen?"

"Allmen. Just Allmen."

"I'm Maria Moreno. Someone told me you were asking for me."

"Thank you for calling."

"Someone recommended me?"

"True."

"Who?"

"A former colleague from Gelbburgstrasse. But she said you might already have a full-time job."

After a short pause she said, "Not anymore. I'm free. But I don't do offices. Only private homes."

"This is private."

"But your card looks like it's from a firm."

"This would be for me at home."

"Full time or by the hour?"

"By the hour."

"I'm looking for full time. With a room."

Allmen hesitated.

"Or by the hour. Would be okay. Thirty."

When Allmen didn't answer straight off, she added, "Or twenty-five. But no lower."

"You can discuss the details with my assistant. I'll give him your information. Just a moment." Allmen turned to the last page of his Chekhov book and took his pen from his jacket. "I'm ready."

"For what?"

"Your details. Name, address, and so on."

"What do you need that for?"

"To pass on to my assistant."

The woman was silent. Then, in a different voice, she said, "I can't work officially though."

"Don't worry. This isn't going any further than my assistant."

Maria Moreno gave Allmen her details. It was only when he asked about her previous employer that she halted. "What do you need to know that for?"

"As a reference, should we need it. Just routine."

She reluctantly gave him the information. "Artyom Sokolov, Spätbergstrasse 19. But you won't get hold of him there."

"Why?"

"He's gone."

"For a long time?"

"Don't know."

"Where?"

"Don't know."

Allmen said goodbye and promised that Señor de Leon would be in touch.

He knew Spätbergstrasse. It was barely five minutes from Villa Schwarzacker by foot.

He put his cellphone back in his inside pocket and waved to Gianfranco for the bill.

While he was waiting he noticed another guest. He was sitting a few tables away, with his back to the wall, like Allmen, reading the *International Herald Tribune*. Allmen was able to observe him in the broad wall-length mirror. At one point the man glanced over the top of his newspaper and their eyes met. Now Allmen noticed his uncanny resemblance to a certain actor. The name was on the tip of his tongue, but he couldn't quite remember.

He turned back to his book, but the actor's name was bothering him. He kept looking back at the man with the newspaper. Next time their eyes met, the man's turned to look past him. Allmen followed his gaze and saw two men sitting at a window table, turned slightly aside.

As he made for the exit after paying, he heard them talking. They were English.

12

The house at Spätbergstrasse 19 was an unfortunate piece of architecture, a 1960s villa built in a mixture of the English and Ticino country house styles. A look without precedent or influence in this district, luckily.

It was built only ten yards from the dense cypress hedge that screened the property from the street. However, this left room for a large garden on the west side, the front of the building. There must have been a fine view of the lake and the mountains from that spot.

The house did not look lived in. The shutters on the ground floor were closed, the windows on the upper floor uncurtained. The lawn on either side of the flagstones to the front door needed a trim, and the mailbox set into the gatepost was overflowing with free magazines and leaflets, despite the sign saying, "Stop! No Adverts!" On the mailbox nameplate someone had written by hand, "A. S."

Allmen pressed the doorbell. Not expecting anything. Just in case.

And who would have thought it: on the top floor, a window opened. A young man in a suit and tie stuck his head out. "Who are you looking for?"

"I have a query about this house."

The man scrutinized Allmen and concluded that this elegant gentleman's query might be of interest. "One moment!" he called, and shut the window.

Shortly afterward he opened the garden gate and came to meet Allmen. He held out his hand and introduced himself as "Schuler."

"Allmen. Pleased to meet you." He gave him his card, the CEO version again.

Schuler cast a glance at it. "Aha. A neighbor, as it were. How can I help you?"

Schuler's short hair was slightly longer at the front and styled into hedgehog spines with gel. He used a rather obtrusive eau de toilette.

"I come past here often and keep seeing the house empty. Is it for sale?"

Schuler shook his head. "Unfortunately not. The property is only to rent."

"Ah. Well, I might consider renting it too. But it would have to be a long-term lease."

"The house is already rented. I'm sorry." Schuler looked genuinely regretful.

"Are you the tenant?"

"No. I'm the agent." He fished a business card from behind his breast-pocket handkerchief and passed it to Allmen. "Immolux," it read, "your specialist for properties in a class of their own. Esteban Schuler, Assistant Vice President."

"But the house doesn't look terribly occupied, Herr Schuler."

Schuler sighed. "It isn't. The tenant never moved in properly."

"What a pity for such a jewel."

They both gazed in sympathy at the neglected house.

"Does he intend to return?" Allmen asked.

"We presume so. The contract runs till the end of the year."

"Perhaps he might be interested in someone to take over the lease. I'd jump at the opportunity."

Schuler looked at the potential client with the promising address. "But you have a very nice residence already."

"Villa Schwarzacker? I would never give that up of course. But it's becoming too small for my company's purposes. What I need is somewhere else to live. Walking distance."

Schuler agreed to a little tour.

In the large vestibule was a furniture delivery, still in its packaging. Otherwise the house was practically empty. In the kitchen were a few cooking implements; in the large salon, a sofa in front of the window, like a look-out bench. In the master bedroom a mattress lay on the floor, with fresh sheets—no doubt the work of Maria Moreno. A suit hung in a plastic moth-proof wardrobe. In the mosaic bathroom there was soap, shower gel, and an unopened tube of tooth-paste with a "two for one" sticker on it.

The distinguishing architectural features of the house

were round brick arches, wrought-iron decorations, imaginative parquet, and decorative stone flooring. Allmen felt like he was on the set of a 1950s music variety show.

The villa had eleven rooms, a sauna, a basement bar with crown glass windows, an automatic bowling alley, a climate-controlled wine cellar, utility rooms, and staff rooms.

The garden contained an artificial grotto with a grill and a fridge. And a kidney-shaped pool, surrounded by rough-hewn granite slabs. The only attractive thing was the view. Over the roofs of the houses farther down the hill, you could look down to the city and the lake in the changing light of the summer's day.

The rent was sixteen thousand francs a month. Excluding service charges. Allmen described the price as fair.

"Let's get right in touch with the tenant today," he suggested.

Schuler turned his palms to the sky, helpless. "If only it were that simple. I don't have a contact address. Neither a postal address nor email. And his cellphone doesn't work. But I promise you, as soon he gets in touch with us, you'll be hearing from me."

13

Allmen loved the smell of freshly mowed lawns. He preferred it to freshly mowed fields. These reminded him of his childhood, the harbinger of the hay season. A sunburned neck, hay dust clinging to it, all itchy.

The scent of freshly mowed lawns did not awaken any bucolic memories. It was an elegant scent. It smelled of manor houses, golf clubs, lawn tennis, and garden parties. Including the ones at the Villa Schwarzacker back in the day, for which Allmen had put up Bedouin tents in case of bad weather, now mothballed in the villa's shed. If Allmen had been a *maître parfumeur*, he would long ago have created a scent called "Lawn."

But on this late afternoon, he would rather have gone without the scent of lawns if he could have talked sooner with the man unleashing it.

Carlos was astride the ride-on mower, taking tantalizingly slow laps although it was past five and his working hours were therefore over. Allmen watched him from the library, saw him emerge from behind the villa, chug up to the north hedge, turn, ride past again, and vanish behind the villa. Carlos remained hidden and Allmen knew it would still be a while till he had cleaned the mower and stowed it away in the shed.

He sat in his leather armchair and pretended to be engrossed in his book. But as soon as he saw Carlos finally approaching the garden house he stood up and went to the vestibule to bump into him by chance.

Carlos arrived in his gray overalls and a cloud of "Lawn" perfume.

He was about to withdraw to change, but Allmen held him back.

"I've been inside."

"No me diga!"

"Sokolov never really lived in the house. Soon after he moved in he went underground."

Allmen told Carlos about his chance meeting with the agent and gave him a detailed description of the house.

When he had finished his report, he asked, "What could make someone who has rented an expensive house, paid for it till the end of the year, and already ordered the furniture, vanish without trace?"

Carlos didn't have to think twice. *"Miedo."*

"Fear? He wasn't afraid to steal a diamond worth forty-five million. Sokolov felt secure. Otherwise he wouldn't have rented that villa. No, no, Sokolov set himself up to live a comfortable, affluent life. But then something happened."

Carlos nodded thoughtfully. "I think so too, Don John. Something happened. Maybe something happened *to him*." He excused himself and climbed the stairs to his quarters.

Before Allmen left the house—the premiere of Bellini's *La Sonnambula* was on his agenda that night—he talked to Carlos again. He was standing in a dark suit in the small hallway waiting for Herr Arnold to ring the bell and take him to the Golden Bar. There he would drink the two margaritas he always drank before the opera. Carlos kept him company while he waited.

"Carlos, I've read that every computer has its own address."

"Sí, Don John. An IP address."

"And with that you can determine the computer's location."

"You can determine the location of the router connecting it to the Internet."

"Why don't you do that, Carlos?"

"I would have to go through his provider, but I don't know who that is. The email address we got from Montgomery doesn't work anymore. Sokolov's email account isn't on that server anymore."

The bell rang. Carlos went to the intercom. "Yes?"

"Taxi," came Herr Arnold's voice.

"Herr von Allmen will be with you in a moment." Carlos opened the door for Allmen and wished him a nice evening.

But Allmen stayed where he was. "What if Sokolov only changed his provider once he got to wherever he is now?"

"Then you could find the IP address via the old provider."

Allmen looked at Carlos encouragingly.

Carlos shook his head. "Only from the administrator of the server."

"Do you know who that is?"

"I could find out."

"And why don't you?"

"An administrator will only give an IP address to the police."

"Ah." Allmen went out into the balmy summer evening.

In less than a quarter of an hour, Carlos knew more about Sokolov's former email server.

Sokolov's address was soko@phinnkka.com; http://www.phinnkka.com was registered in Kolbhausen, a suburb barely fifteen miles away. The server search showed him the location, and he could zoom in so closely he could see the street. It was called Schwarzkirschstrasse, a short cul-de-sac with four houses. In aerial-view mode he could clearly make out each roof.

14

A smell of pig farms and tar: Kolbhausen lay beyond one of the city's eastern hills, with poor transport links and no view of the lake. Schwarzkirschstrasse was part of a small 1960s development of detached houses, surrounded by industrial agriculture, with a small canning factory and a workshop for farm machinery.

Herr Arnold stopped in front of one of the four steep-gabled houses, with espaliered apple trees and hideous garages built at various times over the past fifty years.

It wasn't hard to find the house he was looking for. At the entrance to the second hung an @ symbol instead of a house number. Allmen opened the rusty garden gate. A gravel path led through the overgrown garden to the front door. Above the bell it said "Ernst Neuenhauser." He pressed it. From inside the house came the sound of a roaring lion.

Allmen jumped and stepped back. Nothing happened. Silence except for the rapid dripping of a faucet next to the door, a green plastic bucket overflowing beneath it.

He rang again. Again the roaring lion. Again, nothing happened.

Allmen walked around the house. Most of the garden was filled with abandoned vegetable beds, bolted lettuce, empty beanpoles and tomato supports, overgrown paths between the beds, a collapsing water tank, and a battered, coiled hose in the midst of flourishing nettles.

Three steps led up to the house. The door, which was ajar, had a window with a wrought-iron grill. To the left of it was another window, with a large, empty flower box. Behind it closed curtains. No sign of life.

But just as Allmen was about to look elsewhere, he caught a movement. As if someone had pulled the curtain aside briefly and let it fall again.

Allmen walked toward the three steps, paused for a moment, then climbed them. At the half-open door he stopped. He could hear music, a *Volksmusik* classic.

"Hello?" he called. "Anyone home?" And when he got no reaction, louder: "Excuse me. I'm looking for Herr Neuenhauser!"

It stank of food, cigarettes, and sweat. Allmen stuck his head inside. He saw into a darkened room filled with indescribable chaos. Clothes, grocery bags, pizza boxes, dirty dishes, empty 1.5 liter soda bottles, and iced tea cartons.

Allmen called out again. "Anyone there?" He went inside.

Behind the door he now saw a series of plastic rectangles, probably computer-related. Perhaps this was what servers looked like. Next to them, on an enormous office chair, a very fat, youngish man was facing a row of screens. He didn't seem to have noticed Allmen.

"Grüezi," Allmen said. Then he said it again, louder, *"Grüezi,* Herr Neuenhauser. "

Now the man turned his head and looked at him, suspiciously. "What do you want?"

"Excuse me for barging in like this."

"What do you want?" Neuenhauser was wearing a t-shirt with the slogan, "World Congress on IT 2008." It accentuated every one of his bulges.

"Do you have a moment?"

"No. What do you want?"

"It's about a friend."

Neuenhauser took something colorful out of a cellophane bag, put it in his mouth, and began chewing, as if it were an onerous task.

"I've been trying to contact him for days. Till recently he had a domain registered here. I thought you might be able to help me."

"Are you from the police?"

"No."

"Then I can't help you."

"I understand." Allmen gazed at the large man in silence till he turned his head away.

"What's his name then?"

"Sokolov. Artyom Sokolov."

The man nodded, as if that was exactly what he had expected.

Allmen kept going. "His domain was …" Allmen consulted his stenography notebook. "phinnkka.com."

Neuenhauser stood up. It was as if his bulky body only

followed his nimble movements reluctantly, delayed by fractions of a second.

He walked toward the door. For a moment Allmen thought he was going to leave the room. Then he came back, took the cellophane bag from the desk, and sat on a sagging sofa bed in front of a large TV, the only seat in the room apart from the office chair.

Neuenhauser's face was white and covered in sweat. Allmen wasn't sure if it had been like that before. Had he failed to notice due to the poor lighting by the computers? It was a while before Neuenhauser said anything. "I can't help you. Even if I wanted to."

Allmen sensed an explanation was coming. He waited.

Neuenhauser pointed behind him, without making the effort to turn. "You see the gap under the table there?"

Allmen nodded. In the row of servers, one was missing.

"That was the server with Sokolov's domain on it."

"Where is it now?"

"A few days ago two men came here, English. They wanted to know the same as you. And when I refused to tell them they got rough. I told them the data had been wiped, but they wanted to know which server it was on. And they took it. I guess they want to try and restore it, but they won't succeed. I erase my data securely."

"Why didn't you go to the police?"

Neuenhauser hesitated, then finally said, "I don't want any trouble. I'm not actually responsible for the content of the websites; I just provide the infrastructure. But still, no trouble. You know?"

Allmen knew.

"The very next day two Americans came and asked the same question. I told them about the other two and they left straightaway." Neuenhauser crackled around in his cellophane bag of colorful objects.

"When did you last hear from Sokolov?" Allmen asked.

"That same day, soon after the Americans were here, he called. He wanted to know if I had wiped the data completely. I told him about the two visits."

"What did he say?"

"Nothing. Just hung up."

"And when was that, roughly?"

"I couldn't say roughly. But I can tell you precisely: July ninth."

Allmen only realized now that he was breathing through his mouth to avoid the smell of sweat. "Thank you. And all the best." He turned toward the door. Then he thought of something. "Have you got his number?"

"Yes."

Allmen looked at him till at last he extracted a cellphone from his pants pocket and read out a number.

As soon as Allmen was sat in the back seat of the Cadillac, he called the number.

It was no longer available.

15

They were sitting in the library. Steady summer rain fell on the glass roof. Through one of the open vents they could hear the water splashing from a downspout onto the gravel. Carlos had listened attentively to Allmen's description. Now he said, "You should ask Señor Montgomery about the Englishmen and the gringos."

Allmen nodded. He took his phone, lying on the coffee table, and dialed. Carlos watched as Allmen waited, then left a voicemail, asking to be called back, "urgently, please."

He put the telephone down and looked at Carlos. "Who can they be?"

"Professionals," Carlos said. "Do you think they'll find anything on the server?"

Allmen sighed. "They're always one step ahead of us."

"Not entirely. We know about the house. And we know Maria Moreno."

"That hasn't gotten us very far."

"But they're our best clues. We have to start there."

The phone rang. Allmen answered. It was Montgomery. "What's so urgent?" was his first question.

"Have you hired other investigators?" Allmen asked.

"No. Why do you ask?"

"Because we aren't the only people looking for Sokolov."

Montgomery was silent for a moment. Then he said, "I hope you are the only ones who find him." And hung up.

Allmen looked at the phone in surprise and placed it back on the table.

"*Qué dice?*" Carlos asked.

"No," Allmen replied. "He hasn't hired anyone else."

The rain tapped incessantly on the glass roof.

"Don John?"

"Hm?"

"Do you believe him?"

"Should I?"

Carlos thought about it. "I don't know. I'd prefer it if he were lying."

Allmen nodded. "If they were working for him we needn't be as afraid of them."

"*Ojalá,*" Carlos said—let's hope so.

"And now? What next?"

"Maria Moreno."

16

Maria Moreno was six inches taller than Carlos, and still a short woman. She wore cherry-red lipstick and emphasized the almond shape of her black eyes with powerful eyeliner. When she laughed, a row of snow-white teeth were revealed. But Carlos was granted this pleasure only later.

They had arranged to meet in the restaurant at Kakadu, the department store. At three in the afternoon it was empty except for a handful of pensioners exchanging gossip over coffee and cakes, and a few saleswomen taking a late lunch.

Carlos had called Maria straight after his briefing with Allmen, and introduced himself as Señor von Allmen's assistant. He wanted to discuss the details of a potential position, he said.

She was already there when he arrived, also early. He hadn't identified her at first. From the details Allmen had noted he knew that Maria Moreno was thirty-two, but the only Latina around that age in the Kakadu restaurant looked too pretty for an illegal Colombian cleaning lady, as he imagined. It took over ten minutes, and an increasing amount of eye contact, till Carlos walked over to her table, embarrassed, to ask if she might be Maria Moreno.

During the conversation that followed, Carlos found it difficult to achieve the businesslike tone of a personal assistant interviewing potential employees for his boss. He couldn't help taking a shine to her.

That made it particularly hard to "ask some more detailed questions." This was meant to be his excuse for discovering more about Sokolov's disappearance.

"Very strange that an employer would vanish just like that after such a short time," he suggested.

To which she answered feistily, "Don't you believe me?"

"Of course. Naturally. It was purely an observation. But it's strange, don't you think?"

"But that's just how it happened. The morning before, we had discussed what I'd make for dinner the following evening. And next day he was gone."

Carlos shook his head in sympathy.

"Calf's liver. He asked for calf's liver. I kept it for two days. Then I ate it myself."

"And he never called? Didn't leave so much as a note behind? Didn't say a word about where he was going?"

"Nada. Nada de nada."

"Maybe something happened to him. Maybe he was kidnapped."

This was the moment Carlos first got to admire her white teeth.

"You come from a country with lots of abductions, like

me. Have you ever heard of a kidnapping victim who took a suitcase?"

Carlos smiled too.

Maria Moreno got serious again. "No, no. He went travelling. Before I went to do the shopping, someone from a travel agency called. When I got back, Señor Sokolov was gone."

"Do you remember the name of the travel agency?"

Maria waved for the waiter, annoyed. "What if I did? Are you going to find out where he's travelled to, go after him, and ask if he was satisfied with my work? Or what?"

"No, no. It's nothing to do with the position. I was just curious about his strange behavior. Excuse me."

The waiter arrived at the table.

"The gentleman wishes to pay," Maria Moreno said.

Once Carlos had paid for both their coffees, she said, "So what's the deal with the job? I'll be honest with you. Sokolov was paying me weekly in cash. For one week I paid myself out of the remaining housekeeping money, but when he still hadn't returned by the following Saturday I packed my things and returned my key to the agent. I need work. Urgently."

Carlos searched for a chance to prevent this becoming his last meeting with her.

"I told your boss I could only do full time. But I could work by the hour for now."

And before Carlos could answer, she added, "I said thirty. But I could do it for twenty-five."

Carlos promised to report back very positively on the interview. "The position is pretty much yours. It might have to be just by the hour to begin with. But it's pretty much yours." They arranged to meet the next day, in Kakadu again.

Carlos had just hired a cleaning lady. A luxury neither he nor Allmen could afford. Unless they found the pink diamond.

17

As it did every night, a police patrol car drove at almost a walking pace through the villa district on the hill. On Spät-bergstrasse, the policewoman in the passenger seat had the feeling she'd seen a figure in a spot the headlights' beam hadn't reached.

"Did you see that?"

"What?" The driver hadn't noticed anything.

"Drive slower, and stop when I say."

They drove on fifty yards. At the entrance to number nineteen she ordered, "Stop!"

Nothing to see.

She lowered the window and shone her powerful flashlight at the garden gate. In the fine drizzle nothing moved except the shadows of the gateposts thrown by the flashlight.

The policewoman opened the car door. Her colleague groaned. "What was it? What did you see?"

"I don't know. A figure maybe."

"A fox. Or shadows from our headlights."

The officer got out, walked toward the garden gate, and shone her light around the garden. Nothing.

At her feet was something bright. She pointed the light at it. It was a special-offer leaflet from a wine store. She bent down and picked it up. Across the leaflet was the imprint of a shoe sole.

"Look." She held the evidence up to her colleague.

He rolled his eyes. "Let's go."

She stood for a moment, undecided. Then she went to the mailbox and pushed the leaflet inside.

Carlos waited till the sound of the engine had faded entirely, then crept out of the hedge. His heart was beating so loudly he was worried the policewoman could have heard it. He'd been pressed into the cypress hedge the entire time, the officer just a few inches from him. He had barely been breathing and now he was gasping for air.

If he'd been caught, they'd have taken him to the station to check his ID. That would be the end of his time in Switzerland. He could have boxed his own ears for being so stupid.

Two or three times, as a car approached, he forced himself to walk at a normal speed, then he sped up again. He was using his windbreaker to keep the rain off his loot—the pile of mail Allmen had mentioned in passing.

There was a light coming from the greenhouse. Don John was in his library.

Carlos climbed the stairs and hung his wet jacket on a coat hook. Only now did he notice he was shivering.

He entered the right-hand attic room, which served as his living room. There was just enough space for a table and chair, an upholstered armchair, and a sideboard on which a few mementos of his native country were arranged: two small Maya heads, copies of archeological finds, a carved candle holder, and a few painted gourd bowls. On the wall was a piece of fabric embroidered with birds, and a wooden mask.

He placed the contents of the mailbox on the table and sifted through it: free local magazines, political leaflets, a fishmonger offering home delivery, a new gym opening, changes to the trash collection schedule, introductory prices from a new cleaning service, a poster for a lost tortoise, travel brochures. There were a few envelopes, but they were covered with marketing phrases like, "Do you love vacations?" or "Gourmets, look no further!" or "It's your lucky day!"

One large envelope was stamped with the logo of a travel agency. Someone had written on it, by hand, "No one home. Please call us." Below it, an illegible signature.

From the library came the sound of piano music.

18

Allmen jumped at the knock on the door, so late at night. Since he'd been shot, he'd never felt wholly at ease in his glass library. He had Carlos draw the curtains early, and always sat in different spots.

With the pink diamond case, a different kind of agitation had been added to this nervousness. A kind of constant professional alarm. Hunter's syndrome, he called it.

That night he was having trouble concentrating on his reading. He tried re-reading passages from Bruce Chatwin's *In Patagonia*. Then he put the book aside and turned to the small dossier of Internet research on pink diamonds Carlos had compiled for him. He read about the irregularities in the carbon molecules that in rare cases could color a diamond pink and thus make it twenty times more valuable than normal diamonds. But the rapt attention he usually paid to all things written, whatever the content, was ebbing by the sentence.

He sat down at his Bechstein, whose days with him would have been numbered without the diamond job. He was blundering his way through the Great American Song-book when the knock came, and Carlos entered before Allmen could say "come in."

He walked up to Allmen without a word and handed over his find. "From Sokolov's mailbox," Carlos declared with a flourish.

The top sheet was a memo on the letterhead of a travel agency. Out of the various options, "Further to our telephone conversation" had been ticked. Enclosed was the brochure of a five-star hotel at a snow-white Baltic coast resort on the Bay of Mecklenburg. It was called Le Grand Duc, after the resort's founder, Grand Duke Friedrich Franz I. This was the oldest seaside resort in Germany.

In the margins of the brochure someone had made notes from a telephone conversation. "10 July onward" and "Spätbergstrasse 19" and "Sokolov."

Carlos had reported back on his meeting with Maria Moreno—without mentioning that he had more or less hired her. Allmen knew about the telephone conversation with the travel agency, and the suitcase Sokolov had taken with him.

"On July tenth," he noted. "The day after he got the call saying the Brits had taken the server."

Carlos nodded. "Over a month ago."

"Maybe he's still there. And if not, maybe they have some information about where he is now. I'll have no choice but to do some research on site." He didn't manage to make his sigh convincing.

Carlos said nothing. But Allmen knew the budgetary

aspect of this business trip would be worrying him.

"We'll have to ask Montgomery for a second payment," Allmen added.

When Carlos still said nothing, Allmen got up and went to the telephone. "Unless he possesses a fake ID or credit card, he'll have been forced to check in under his real name." He dialed the number on the brochure.

Carlos heard him speak in English, "Mr. Sokolov, please."

Allmen held his hand over the receiver and nodded to Carlos, excited. After a short while he said, still in English, "I see. Never mind. No, thank you, no message. Goodbye."

He looked at Carlos, triumphant. "Not in his room."

19

Allmen had already heard great things about the establishment, and the midnight-blue Bentley Mulsanne that picked him up from Rostock Airport seemed to confirm its good reputation.

The upholstery was taupe leather, the interior veneered in redwood burl, the driver silent and uniformed, steering the vehicle with the assurance and care of an elderly aristocrat's chauffeur.

Allmen enjoyed the journey from Rostock to Heiligendamm. He leaned back and took in the avenues slipping past, interrupted from time to time by homesteads with heavy thatch roofs. Right now the profession of investigator was very much to his taste.

At the Grand Duc he was welcomed like a longtime regular. The general manager had been informed when the Bentley entered the hotel grounds and was waiting for Allmen in the lobby. He expressed his conviction that the weather would improve by the following day and accompanied his guest to the reception desk, where he placed him in the care of a colleague.

The receptionist had filled in the registration form already, leaving Allmen just to sign it. It was only when she asked to make an impression of his credit card that a slight hiccup occurred in the smooth reception process.

"Credit card?" Allmen asked in amazement. "I have never owned a credit card and will never own such a thing." He displayed his most charming of smiles. "But I take it you also accept real money?"

The receptionist returned his smile, but asked to be excused for a second and vanished into the office behind the desk. Shortly afterward she returned, smiling again. She made no further mention of the credit card. "Shall I show you to your suite now?"

On the way to the elevator, Allmen confirmed this was his first visit to the Grand Duc. In the elevator he assured her his journey had been pleasant and he wasn't too tired from the exertions. In the corridor he asserted he was reassured by the prospect the weather would improve. And in the suite he expressed satisfaction with the latter.

In that instance there really was no cause for complaint. It included a generous bedroom with en suite bath, a separate toilet, a walk-in closet, and a large salon with a view of the Baltic Sea and the beach with its wicker chairs. Allmen had decided on the highest category of accommodation. He saw no reason why he should stay more modestly at the firm's expense than he would at his own.

Carlos had already mailed an invoice for the second payment to Montgomery the day before, due upon receipt. The reason: costs incurred during extended research. Where this was taking place, he had not specified. If there was any connection between Montgomery and the other investigators, he didn't want to jeopardize this potential head start.

Allmen anticipated the payment would appear at any moment in the firm's account. So he had no reason for financial worries and planned to mix business with pleasure.

20

Never, during his countless travels, had he experienced the sea like this. Such mighty calm, such guarded promise, a mysterious symbiosis of the northern and southern.

Although the sky was cloudy, the climate was mild, gentle, inviting, damp, almost tropical. Only the light was different. More serious, more ceremonious.

A long jetty stretched out into the water, like a bridge to a vanished shore. He could see a few people on it, walking in both directions, slowly, like passengers on a ship who want to draw out their departure or arrival.

Without even unpacking his suitcase or filling the closet, he put on his swimming trunks, slipped into a bathrobe, and walked to the beach. Only a few of the canopied wicker beach chairs were occupied.

He threw the white robe with the hotel crest onto the fine sand and approached the water.

It wasn't as cold as it looked, and he walked into it on a carpet of sand so soft there was enough time for his body to get accustomed to the cool.

Only when he was out of his depth did he start swimming. And only when he had swum beyond the far end of the jetty did he turn.

He looked at the beach, the tall chairs, the parasols, and the snow-white palatial hotels.

Somewhere there was the man he was searching for.

PART 2

21

Next day the weather was even worse. Out of habit, Allmen had ordered a cup of tea in bed at 7:00 a.m. The room waiter advised him it might be better to stay there.

Two hours later he was woken by gusts of rain battering the windows.

The swallows, normally in constant flight, providing for their young, were sitting fluffed up by their nests on the small tower designed for them, waiting for the rain to stop.

Last night, Allmen had ordered an early supper in his room. Afterward, he had sauntered through the hotel complex, discreetly checking the various restaurants, the lobby, the smoking room, the library, and the bar. He saw no one resembling Sokolov. Had he moved on now?

After his tour, he called Carlos and asked him to telephone the hotel and request to speak with Sokolov. A few minutes later Carlos called back with the information that Herr Sokolov was away for the night, expected back tomorrow. Relieved, Allmen went to bed and slept wonderfully.

After his early morning tea, he ordered breakfast in his room: *milchkaffee*, croissants with butter and honey, scrambled egg with ham, and a little smoked eel. A nutritious meal. Later he planned to emulate the hardy types he could see down on the beach, leaping into the breakers despite the weather.

At ten he called Carlos. Allmen knew he was on a morning shift today and would switch on his phone at this time. He took his break at ten. Like every Hispanic person throughout the world.

Carlos was, *"Sin novedad, gracias a Dios,"* an expression from his native Guatemala, where news tended to be bad: without news, thank God.

Carlos had heard nothing from Montgomery, which to Allmen implied he had accepted the second payment request. However, no money had appeared yet. Carlos assured him he planned to check the balance on the Allmen International account at lunchtime again.

Soon after their call, the rain eased off. Allmen packed his beach hamper, a wicker shopping basket lined with plastic and sporting the hotel emblem. He put his trunks on, a pair of washed-out chinos on top, and wearing a sweatshirt with the Charterhouse crest and his much-loved Barbour jacket, freshly waxed by Carlos before the trip, he left the suite.

In the corridor he met the housekeeper, a tall, bony woman in her mid-forties. "Smudgy day," she said.

Allmen didn't understand.

"It's raining from north, south, east, and west," she said.

"Aha. And that's known as smudgy?"

"By me it is."

In Allmen's hotel experience, housekeepers were almost as important as concierges and maîtres d'hôtel. If you got on the right side of them, your room was always clean, little wishes were granted, your washing returned from the laundry swiftly, your suits were brushed and ironed out, your tissue box full, and your bathrobe fresh each day. Allmen inquired after her name, gave her a hundred euro tip, and wished her a not too smudgy day.

She was called Frau Schmidt-Gerold. He noted the name.

The gate to the beach was locked. Only when the idle beach attendant rushed to his assistance did Allmen realize that it opened with his keycard.

He had a beach chair set up for him, got comfortable, and gazed at the sand, watching the gulls.

For a long while they remained immobile. All of a sudden, they flew up, screeching, described inscrutable figures, then settled back down, immobile again.

Occasionally they scuttled along the edge of the surf, looking for edible jetsam as the water retreated.

In the distance he made out three container vessels. A trawler, closer by. The little catamaran from the hotel's sailing school launched from the beach; on board were a few children in enormous, fluorescent life jackets.

A thinner bundle of cloud hung from the dark-gray bank that blocked the pale-gray clouds beyond.

Allmen took a book from the beach basket and began to read: *The House on the Strand*, by Daphne du Maurier.

An hour later he was suddenly pulled out of Maurier's delightful time-travel story back to the present. It took him a moment to register what it was.

A man's voice, speaking Russian.

22

Now he noticed the weather had improved. It had stopped raining, the wind had died down, and the dense cloud was even letting occasional rays of sunshine through.

Allmen stood in front of his beach chair and looked around. Quite a few other hotel guests were on the beach now. Many had turned their chairs around so the few rays of sun didn't simply hit their back, as in Allmen's case. Children were playing in the sand, and a few of the tables at the beach bar were occupied.

The Russian voice was directly behind him. It didn't sound like a forty-year-old; it must belong to an old man, sedately describing times gone by.

Allmen listened. Military ranks came into it, and expressions such as billet, field kitchen, officer's mess, sentry, inspection; the old man was describing military service. And soon Allmen realized he was talking about the time when the Grand Duc had been requisitioned by the Red Army and, as a young officer, he had enjoyed what he called the best part of the war.

The other man's voice sounded younger. But it was limited to monosyllabic comments and expressions of admiration, surprise, and astonishment.

Allmen walked between the wicker chairs toward the beach bar. This gave him the chance to glimpse the speaker. He was a very pale man, his ample body filling both seats of the chair. He had leaned his head back, and was looking with half-closed eyes down at the man crouched on the sand in front of him.

The listener had his back to Allmen, who couldn't see his face. But his hair was thin and mousy-blond.

At the beach bar Allmen ordered a glass of champagne. To calm his racing heart.

He could only see the back of beach chair thirty-two. Allmen kept his eye on it. On his way back he would take another route to get a glance at the listener.

After the second glass his heart stopped racing and the mixture of euphoria and recklessness had set in, for which he so loved the drink.

He signed the bill and gave the barman a tip large enough to help him remember Allmen's name and room number. Then he wandered back to his chair.

The old man was still telling stories. But the listener was no longer crouching. Now he was standing up. He was a short man, nowhere near Sokolov's six foot two. His face was rounded and his eyes were not sunken.

Allmen sat back down in his chair and returned to his reading.

After a while the beach attendant began preparing the neighboring chair, opening it up, removing the wooden cover, pulling out the footrests, brushing the sand off.

"Thank you," the guest accompanying him said. "Please bring me a *milchkaffe*."

His accent made Allmen look up.

The man was tall, with a narrow face and thin, dark-blond hair, combed back, and deep-set eyes.

23

Only twelve days after receiving the assignment, Allmen International Inquiries had found the man they were charged with looking for.

Allmen would dearly have liked to impress his client with this success immediately. But he had to be patient. Naturally he wanted to discuss the situation with Carlos first.

Allmen took his trousers and sweatshirt off and entered the water. He swam for a while, till he felt he could walk back to his chair, watching Sokolov, without giving the impression that was the only reason he had gone swimming.

Sokolov was sitting sideways in his chair with his legs drawn up. He had a small laptop on his knees and was typing. As Allmen passed him he looked up quickly then focused straight back on his screen.

Allmen dried his hair, peering from under his towel as he did so. Sokolov was not dressed for swimming. His skin showed no sign of having been at a beach resort for over a month. He looked harmless. Harmless and a little lonely.

Another hour till he could call Carlos. He spent it reading, just two yards from the man who—if everything went to plan—would help him earn 1.8 million francs.

Twenty minutes too early, Allmen packed his beach basket. In passing he nodded to his new neighbor, who had pulled the awning down as low as it would go and failed to look up from his laptop.

"Now that it's finally nice, you're leaving?" the beach attendant said in amazement. Allmen gave him a tip and asked him to reserve chair seventeen for him for the duration of his stay.

At ten past twelve on the dot he called home.

"Allmen International," Carlos answered, with his Hispanic accent.

"I've got him, Carlos," Allmen announced.

"*Felicitaciones!*"

Allmen briefly described how he had found him, that by chance they were beach chair neighbors, and the impression Sokolov made on him.

"Montgomery said, 'When you've found him, follow him and let us know. Then we'll discuss the next stage.'"

They were silent. Both thinking the same thing. It was Allmen who said it out loud.

"We don't really trust him, do we, Carlos?"

"No, Don John."

"Has the money been transferred?"

"Unfortunately not, Don John."

"See what I mean?"

"*Una sugerencia, nada más.*"

"Yes?"

"We inform him that we've found him. But we don't say where."

Allmen thought it through. The idea appealed to him. That way he could find out how Montgomery wanted to proceed, without the risk of him snatching the booty. "Yes, let's do it."

"But ... Don John?"

"Yes?"

"You have to switch your cellphone off and stop using it. Phones can be located."

"Then it's better if *you* inform Montgomery, Carlos."

Allmen ended the conversation and switched the phone off. He lay on his bed, crossed his arms behind his head, and contemplated how he was going to shadow Sokolov with a team of one.

The swallows' polyvocal chirping and the gulls' occasional laughter lulled him to sleep.

Fifteen minutes later, when he woke, refreshed, he had an idea.

He showered and dressed for lunch. Then he called Frau Schmidt-Gerold, the housekeeper, to his room with the excuse that he wanted another cushion for reading on the recamier. He backed the request up with a fifty euro note, which the woman almost refused to accept.

She had nearly left the room before he asked what he really wanted. "Oh, Frau Schmidt-Gerold, could I ask you just one little favor?"

"Certainly, Herr von Allmen."

"Could you just pop this in Herr Sokolov's room for

me?" He held out an unaddressed, sealed envelope, with the hotel crest on it. "You know, Herr Sokolov from room …"

"Two-one-four."

Allmen withdrew his hand. "Actually, on second thought, no, I'll see him myself in a moment at lunch."

Frau Schmidt-Gerold assured him she would happily do this favor, but Allmen said he'd changed his mind.

Room 214 must be on the same floor as his, and sure enough, there it was, on the fire escape plan hanging in his walk-in wardrobe. It was a suite like his, with the same layout. There was just one difference. It had a small bay window.

He passed by reception on the way to lunch. The receptionist who had welcomed him on arrival was on duty now.

"Good day, Herr von Allmen. I hope you're enjoying your stay with us."

"It's perfect, thank you," Allmen confirmed, "almost perfect."

"*Almost?*"

"Well it's just a detail really. I noticed room two hundred fourteen has a small bay window. Could you check if it's free for me?"

The receptionist went to the computer and returned, full of regret, with the news that the room was occupied.

"Could you tell me till when?"

She returned to the screen and regretted to inform him that the guest had not stated a departure date. "Is there anything else I can do for you?"

"Yes, please let me know as soon as you have a checkout date. Would you do that for me?"

She promised to put a note in the file for 214. As soon as she or her colleagues were given a departure date, he would be informed.

Allmen pushed a hundred euro note over the counter and expressed his heartfelt thanks.

The weather was fine enough for lunch on the terrace, which was full of wealthy people in leisure wear. They wore a lot of blue-green, stripes, and polo shirts, with emblems, insignia, and hand-sized polo players on the breast.

Sokolov was there too. He was sitting in the shade of the veranda, where there were hardly any other guests. He had eyes only for his laptop, occasionally forking some food into his mouth.

Allmen stayed till Sokolov signed the bill and stood up. He followed him and saw him disappear into the elevator. The display panel indicated the second floor, then went out. Allmen called the elevator down to the ground floor and likewise went up to the second floor. When he walked past room 214 the "Do Not Disturb" sign was hanging over the handle.

Allmen went to his room and sat in the armchair by the window, reading and wandering down the corridor every half hour.

The sign remained on Sokolov's door throughout the afternoon.

24

He saw him next in the dining room.

Sokolov was sitting at a four-person corner table from where he had a view of the whole room.

Allmen had been given the exact same table in the corner diagonally opposite.

Sokolov was the only man in the dining room not wearing a tie. He hadn't needed such a good table; throughout his meal he stared at his small laptop.

And that, even though the food was amazing. Allmen had chosen the tasting menu, something he often did at the start of an extended stay in a hotel. It was more than just a vote of confidence in the chef; it also gave him an overview of his or her strengths and weaknesses.

He could barely find a weakness however. Not when it came to fish—baked sole with artichokes sautéed and steamed in olive oil then deglazed with white wine. Nor poultry—corn-fed chicken cooked in a Dutch oven with caramelized bacon and vegetables. Nor meat—breaded flank of veal with sage and anchovy beignets.

The wine menu was also very respectable. He even found

his favorite red from the Priorat region, Clos Martinet 1993. A joy at a very decent price of 260 euros for such a rarity.

So no weaknesses. But a notable strength when it came to desserts. The buffet held an array of nougat chocolate creations, baked pineapple in a crispy shell, lemon tartlets, vanilla profiteroles, a number of mille-feuilles, *crêpe* parcels, strudel cakes, soufflés, *gâteaux*, *crèmes* and a breathtaking range of sorbets.

Allmen would have enjoyed a greater sense of contentment, which fine food and drink in a pleasant atmosphere normally brought him, if he hadn't had to keep paying attention to his surveillance object.

However, Sokolov hardly demanded his full attention. He was concentrating on his laptop as ever, shoveling the culinary works of art into his mouth without a thought. A typical IT person.

But once, as Allmen took one of his regular monitoring glances, Sokolov had turned away from his computer and was looking back at him. Their eyes met, and Sokolov nodded.

Allmen nodded back and returned to his plate.

25

Sokolov was not at breakfast the next morning. Allmen made a tour of the hotel complex, but he was nowhere to be seen. He suspected he was on the beach, but before he got there a sudden shower drove the bathers away. He fled to his room, sat at the window, and gazed at the overcast sky and the beach, empty of people.

The solitary beach attendant was closing up the beach chairs and collecting towels. He stood still at one of the chairs. He looked as if he was talking to someone. Then he walked on.

Against the smoke-gray sky was a lighter bank of clouds from which curtains of rain hung, far off, over the sea.

Suddenly, from among the rows of beach chairs, aligned with military precision, a tall, white, monastic figure emerged. It was a man in a hotel bathrobe. He had the hood pulled down over his face and was heading for the spa. Calmly, unconcerned by the pouring rain.

Allmen put his trunks on and cloaked himself in a toweling robe to walk downstairs and out briefly through the rain to the spa.

Here too his keycard opened the door. He found himself in a warm reception area smelling of essential oils. The light was subdued and came from the illuminated entrances to the saunas, changing rooms, steam baths, and massage rooms.

Another entrance led to the pool area. Allmen was met by the moist warmth of the heated swimming pool, a mild aroma of chlorine, and the shouts of children. It was a busy time. Clearly most of the guests driven off the beach by the rain had come here. Allmen found the last free lounger and got comfortable. He returned to Daphne du Maurier's time-travel adventure, but continually broke off reading to observe the guests.

There were several families of three generations there—couples with their children and their parents. Fathers whose unnatural manner of horsing around with their kids suggested that they didn't normally spend much time with them. And there were some who were rich enough not to have to look good—overweight, flaccid, and unfit, but satisfied with themselves and the world.

Next time Allmen looked up from his book, he saw Sokolov. He was standing at the entrance removing his soggy bathrobe, which he threw in the basket for used towels, before going to the shower.

He was a very white, very lean man. Above the drawstring on his long white Bermudas a straight dark line rose to his breastbone where it split like the highest point of a fountain into strange, symmetrical chest hair.

Sokolov stayed a long time under the warm jet, his head thrown back, eyes closed, like someone who wants to rinse the ordeals of the day from his body.

Then he went to the pool and slid into the water. Allmen only realized how blatantly he was watching him when their eyes met. Sokolov nodded to him. This time he smiled a little. Allmen smiled back.

Sokolov started swimming. Allmen headed for the warm Jacuzzi, separated from the pool by a narrow wall. A few kids in armbands were splashing around in it, under the watchful eyes of their parents. Allmen sat up to his neck in the frothing water and peered over the edge of the Jacuzzi toward the pool, where Sokolov was systematically doing his laps.

Suddenly he lost sight of him. Allmen stood up and waded to the edge of the Jacuzzi. There, right below him, stood Sokolov, talking with a man. Allmen immediately retreated to his original spot. It was a while before Sokolov was back in his field of vision, swimming again. On the steps to the pool he saw the man who had been listening so attentively to the fat Russian's war stories. Was this a chance encounter of two countrymen? Or two accomplices making contact?

26

She had intense red hair with a shimmer of gold. There was an almost bluish tint to her white skin. Her breezy, low-hung dress and thin shawl were different shades of green. Her toenails were painted a shade of red that jarred with her hair. She looked as if she was constantly forced to prevent herself and everything around her from being blown to the four winds. She was young, but you could already sense the marks age would one day leave on her. When she lay in the sun, she covered herself entirely with a beach towel, focusing on a Sudoku book and moving her lips as she worked through it. She wore a lot of gold around her wrists and on her fingers. The frames of her sunglasses were also gold trimmed.

Allmen had been watching her for a long time from his beach chair. She had shown no sign she was aware of his gaze. She could easily have evaded it by sitting in her chair instead of using it solely as base camp.

Her companion was somewhat older and stayed mostly in the chair. Allmen saw him briefly as he wandered toward the bar. The man was on the phone, writing in a large notebook. He was stocky, with a moustache, and fully clothed like his partner. His only concession to beach life was his foot-wear; his lumpy, naked white feet were strapped into sandals.

Allmen nodded to him, as he seemed to be looking in his direction. But he was checking in on the woman.

"Vanessa!"

Vanessa? Allmen savored the name and decided it suited her.

He carried on to the bar and ordered his light snack—strawberries with cream and a glass of champagne. From here he could easily keep an eye on Sokolov's beach chair.

Aside from his conversation with the other Russian, Sokolov had done nothing further out of the ordinary. He ate his dinner in the dining room, accompanied by a beer, and never looked away from his laptop if he could help it. He divided his time between the beach, the pool, and his room.

Allmen found it easy to adjust to Sokolov's rhythm. He got lots of reading done, took advantage of the excellent cuisine and the wine menu, full of constant surprises, and didn't even have to forgo his siesta, even if it was sometimes disturbed or curtailed. Sokolov was not a difficult surveillance subject. And if he did ever lose sight of him briefly, he could rely on the reception team, who would undoubtedly inform him straightaway of the impending departure of the guest in suite 214.

He called Carlos from the phone in his room now. Last time they had talked the money was still not in their account. It was on its way, Montgomery had said. A sentence Allmen did not like to hear. He had used it too often himself.

Carlos also reported that Montgomery had taken the news they had found Sokolov entirely as a matter of course. He had accepted that Carlos didn't want to say where he was, and instructed them to continue shadowing Sokolov. He would inform them about the next move.

"The next move" was a subject at the top of Allmen's mind. Right now he didn't have the slightest idea.

But after three days without developments, things took their own course.

27

A fresh southeasterly had swept in and banished the clouds lurking ominously over the hotel palaces all morning. The change of weather caught the staff off guard, and they were still setting up the beach bar for good weather as the first guests arrived.

The sea, which just a minute ago had been splashing gently back and forth, now sent real waves ashore. Not breakers, but large enough to animate the gulls, who until then had been standing in lines along the breakwaters watching for pickings.

Vanessa was lying on a towel a few feet away from him, covered to her chin, working on her Sudoku. Allmen gazed at her, lost in thought.

Suddenly she let her book fall and looked straight at him. Too late for Allmen to avert his gaze and pretend he hadn't been watching her. He had no choice but to give her a sheepish smile.

Vanessa beamed back.

He was still wondering how he should react, as hers was not the kind of smile you could respond to simply with a further smile, when a shadow fell over him. It was Sokolov's.

There he stood, in brand-new, ill-fitting jeans and a polo shirt, not yet laundered, still with creases on its short sleeves.

"Nice at last," he said.

"Indeed," Allmen replied.

Sokolov bridged the looming silence with, "Have you been here before?"

"No, my first time." Allmen stood up and held out his hand. "Allmen."

"Sokolov," the diamond thief of the century said, and gave his observer a friendly smile. Normally Allmen would now have offered him a chair. He looked at the two-person space on his beach chair and said, "I can hardly offer you this seat."

"Thanks," Sokolov said, and sat down on it.

Allmen had no choice but to sit next to him.

The wind carried voices over from the water, scattered shouts, children's cries and laughter, drowned by the surf, reminding Allmen of the carefree swimming-pool afternoons of his childhood.

He was about to ask, "You're Russian, right?" in Russian, but at the last minute decided it was more prudent to stick to German. Perhaps it would be useful if Sokolov didn't know he understood his language.

"And I thought I spoke German without an accent. And you—let me guess?"

Sokolov didn't need more than one try. It was easy to guess. Although Allmen could speak accent-free German, he left this at home when travelling to Germany, taking instead his Swiss accent. It made a better impression.

"I'm often in Switzerland," Sokolov disclosed, "for work."

"What do you do?"

"IT."

"I thought so."

"Does it show?"

"The laptop. Your constant companion."

"Ah, I see. And you? What do you do?"

They had come to Allmen's favorite question.

"I'm a man of independent means."

Most people registered this statement with awe. But Sokolov wasn't familiar with the expression. "So what does that involve?" he asked.

"A bit of this, a bit of that."

"I see. You're free to do whatever currently earns most."

Allmen shook his head. "Whatever currently interests me most."

"That's my career goal too."

The pendants on the small awning above the chair rustled in the wind, accompanied by the laughter of the gulls who suddenly flew up, as if obeying a secret command, and followed their inscrutable paths.

And again Allmen met Vanessa's gaze. It seemed she had been looking over at him throughout the two men's exchange, waiting to see how he would respond to her inviting smile. He decided to raise his eyebrows and shoulders in a gesture of helplessness.

"Are you eating in the hotel again tonight?" Sokolov's question sounded like an attempt to revitalize the conversation.

"Yes. The food there is excellent, I find." And then All-men said it: "Would you like to join me at my table?"

They arranged to meet at 8:00 p.m. in the bar.

28

Allmen was there a little earlier, as always when meeting people. A gesture of politeness originally intended for ladies, which he had long since extended to men.

He drank a Singapore Gin Sling, which he'd asked the barman to make with a shade less Cointreau and grenadine and more Angostura bitters. A trick the bartender at Raffles in Singapore had shared with him. It made the drink slightly drier.

After the beach he'd tried to call Carlos from his room. He wanted to report back on the latest developments. But then something unusual happened. A Hispanic woman's voice answered. "Casa von Allmen," she said.

Allmen was taken aback, stated his name and asked if Herr de Leon was available.

"Carlos *está ocupado,* señor von Allmen," she responded. Carlos was busy.

Only now did Allmen inquire with whom he had the pleasure.

"Maria Moreno," she answered, almost reproachfully. She explained that Carlos was still working in the garden.

Allmen asked what she herself was doing.

Her reply sounded incredulous. "Cleaning."

Allmen took his drink and sat by the large window alongside the bar.

The sea lay dark and heavy. Against the clear, blue-black evening sky a garland of white clouds had formed.

Allmen heard the barman say "Good evening." He assumed Sokolov had arrived, and turned toward the bar.

But it was not the man he was waiting for. Two men he hadn't seen here before were there. One looked familiar.

Suddenly Allmen remembered where he'd seen him last: in Café Viennois. He'd been sitting at a table by the wall reading the *Herald Tribune*. He'd been able to observe him in the mirror. He resembled an American actor. Then, as now, he couldn't remember the name.

The two men were chatting, loud and unself-consciously, in American English. They were ordering cocktails and took no notice of him. Allmen was sure it was the same man.

His heart raced. An American he had noticed in Viennois was now at a luxury hotel on the Baltic coast. That couldn't be a coincidence.

Sokolov came in. He was wearing a tie, probably so he didn't stand out next to Allmen, who arrived elegantly dressed for dinner every evening.

He ordered a vodka. "No point pretending I'm not Russian," he observed. "And what are you drinking?"

"Singapore Gin Sling. The sea here reminds me of that area."

"It reminds me of my childhood. Same sea, a bit farther north."

If from a distance Sokolov had seemed to Allmen like a cagey loner, close up he turned out to be open and direct. He described the youth camps near Tallinn he was sent to as a child, the military manner in which they were run. Allmen offered a few stories from Charterhouse, the exclusive boarding school where he had spent his youth, painting it as more militaristic than the reality.

When they walked through to the dining room, the man who resembled the actor was still deep in conversation with his companion. At the table, Sokolov asked, "Did you see the American? Looks like Martin Sheen."

For the hors d'œuvre they ordered eel, not a rarity as such in the region. But the preparation was unusual: it followed a recipe from the Camargue, glazed in red wine sauce.

As Allmen was singing its praises, Sokolov surprised him with another revelation. "I've got no idea about food. Till now I've only ever eaten to fill my stomach. It's something I have to learn."

"You don't mean to say it doesn't matter to you what you eat?" Allmen asked incredulously.

"Not saying it doesn't matter, but it's not important."

"Well perhaps you're right," Allmen concurred without conviction. "Perhaps people place too much emphasis on food." He took a sip of wine. "And how do you feel about wine? That doesn't matter either?"

"Not really. I'm a vodka drinker. You don't drink vodka for gastronomic reasons." He put his wineglass to his lips, held a sip in his mouth awhile, and attempted to feel something. "As I said, I still have lots to learn. Everything really:

eating, drinking, clothes, travelling, living, taste … Being rich, basically."

Allmen was still searching for an appropriate answer as Sokolov added, "Someone like you who learned all that in the cradle wouldn't understand, of course."

Allmen didn't disabuse him. "Don't worry, you'll soon catch up. You seem to have one of the most important prerequisites already."

"Which one?"

"Money. Being rich is easier if you have money."

Sokolov laughed, not guessing how much that sentence rang true for Allmen. "I'm still in an experimental phase. And the money is just a foretaste too."

They enjoyed a pleasant, relaxed, and increasingly amusing evening. They were the last guests in the dining room and the only ones to drink another for the road on the terrace. And another.

They talked in lowered voices, allowing ever longer pauses. Gazed out at the sea. At the avenue of lamps along the promenade. Into the sparkling summer night sky. At the fluorescing crests of the delicate waves.

It was after midnight when they finally left the terrace, and the man who had been watching them from a balcony put down his binoculars and said a few words into his earpiece.

Outside Sokolov's room, Allmen asked, "How long do you plan to stay?"

"Not sure. As long as I want to."

"There we go, you're getting the hang of being rich."

29

Allmen showered, brushed his teeth, and put on clean pajamas. But once he was in his bedroom, he realized he wouldn't be able to sleep. Too many thoughts running around in his head.

Why was the American from Viennois here? Was there a connection between him and Sokolov? Was he one of the Americans who had turned up at the apartment building, the rental agency, Lonely Nights, and the server administrator's house?

And if so, why was he in Viennois? Was there some link between the American and him, Allmen?

Was he shadowing him?

Allmen did something he never normally did after drinking so much; he rounded off the evening with one last beer. He took a Pilsner from the minibar, filled a glass, and sat in the armchair by the window.

Assuming Montgomery was having him watched, was he doing it to protect himself? Was he hedging his bets?

It seemed all the more likely these people were working for Montgomery. That would also explain why he hadn't insisted they disclose Sokolov's whereabouts. He knew them already.

And what about Sokolov? He had said his life as a rich man was still in a trial phase, the money itself just a foretaste. Both facts pointed to the pink diamond. He, or the gang he belonged to, hadn't yet cashed in the diamond. Sokolov was enjoying his wealth in advance. The villa in Spätbergstrasse, the housekeeper, the suite at the Grand Duc were all in anticipation of the bonanza to come. On borrowed money. Or perhaps saved.

Their kindred spirit—both living in style on money they didn't possess—made him warm to Sokolov. It made him doubt if he was dealing with a real criminal here. He could just about imagine a computer nerd stealing a diamond worth forty-five million. But the stone vanished at a party hosted by its multi-millionaire owner. How could someone like Sokolov have gained access to such circles?

Perhaps he hadn't actually been there. It was unlikely such an enormous coup was the work of a lone wolf. Much more likely to involve a gang. With Sokolov simply a member. Perhaps the brains? Perhaps the computer expert?

Allmen had to get access to Sokolov's suite. Perhaps he would find a clue there. Exonerating him perhaps.

He finished his beer, brushed his teeth again, and looked out one last time at the nighttime sea.

Far, far out, a cruise liner sailed past. A pattern of filigreed light.

30

Almost blue, the bank of cloud on the horizon looked like a lakeside landscape. As if Allmen were sitting by a large, peaceful lake and the sailboats were drifting past the opposite shore.

Getting up had been harder than usual. His brain was fuzzy, how he felt after too little sleep and too much alcohol. A quick dip in the cool Baltic Sea had revived him a little, but now the salt water had dried on his skin and his whole body felt sticky. He was too lazy to walk the few feet to the shower, close to the beach bar.

Sokolov's beach chair was empty. He probably felt as rough as Allmen. But Vanessa and her companion were there. The man was working away at his business as usual. But this time, instead of lying on the sand, Vanessa was walking up and down the beach holding a bright children's bucket, her eyes glued to the ground. Every so often she bent down to pick up a seashell, examined it, and either threw her find in the bucket or back on the beach.

She was wearing the low-cut dress again, with lots of

green, and the shawl that protected her delicate skin from the sun. And a large straw hat.

Allmen looked up from his book toward her from time to time. She acted as if she were totally absorbed in her shell hunt and hadn't noticed him. Every time Allmen glanced at her, she had inched closer toward him.

Next time it wasn't as easy to look back down. Vanessa was standing a few yards away from him, bending forward. She had opened her shawl, and the dress offered a good view of her cleavage. She stayed like this for what seemed like an eternity, then she crouched down. Her knees now hid her cleavage, but the dress had slid up her legs. It was impossible to avoid noticing she had nothing on underneath.

Suddenly she looked up and met his gaze. Allmen looked back down at his book, but he could feel her eyes on him. He looked up again. She was still squatting in the same position, but now she was smiling at him provocatively. He smiled back and shifted his gaze a little lower.

For a moment they stayed fixed like this.

"Vanessa!"

It was her companion's voice. She stood up in her own time, and left.

At this point Sokolov arrived. Allmen wasn't sure if he'd observed the scene. If he had, he let nothing show. He said good morning, began sorting out his beach chair, turned it to face Allmen, and sat down. "Are you feeling as hungover as I am?"

"The sea. The sea will help."

"Sometimes what helps me is the sauna."

Allmen pulled a face. "With me that makes it worse."

Sokolov turned to his laptop and Allmen to his book. Helene von Nostitz, *Stories from Old Europe*, almost the perfect book for this location.

But he couldn't concentrate on the past. He was too pre-occupied with the present. Above all the issue of how he could get his hands on Sokolov's keycard.

Vanessa and her companion were leaving. She gave him no further look. The man put a proprietary arm around her shoulder, then they turned their backs on Allmen and walked slowly toward the hotel.

Suddenly she removed her hand from his waist and put it behind her back. She made a fist, then opened and closed it three times in a swift, furtive wave.

Allmen's thoughts soon returned to Sokolov's keycard. Now he had an idea.

"What about this for a compromise. You go to the sauna, I'll go in the sea, then we meet in an hour at the bar in the spa and I'll invite you for a pick-me-up."

Sokolov looked up in surprise, snapped his laptop shut, and stood up. "A deal," he said simply, packed his beach bag, and left.

Allmen stood up and went into the water. It felt cool and soft, and was sending gentle waves ashore.

He looked back and saw Sokolov retreating in his white bathrobe.

Two other figures, also wearing hotel bathrobes, now left the beach bar. They were new arrivals whom Allmen had first noticed on his way past the bar toward his chair. Two Brits with shaved heads, who didn't look like they could afford a hotel like this.

They went the same way as Sokolov.

31

Allmen gave Sokolov ten minutes' head start. Then followed him into the spa.

In the pool it was quieter than usual. The weather was nice enough for the children to play in the sand, which was still damp from the morning's light rain, malleable like spring snow.

Allmen went past the pool to the corridor leading to the sauna area. He entered the relaxation room, lit only by soft LEDs in changing colors. Restful Indian music emanated from somewhere.

The room was empty apart from two men. One was lying on a lounger, apparently asleep. The other was standing next to a different lounger, on which lay a towel, bathrobe, and beach basket. On Allmen's arrival, he stepped quickly away from it and lay on the one next to the sleeping man.

Now Allmen recognized them. It was the two Brits.

He could see the glint of Sokolov's silvery laptop poking out of the beach basket. He settled down on the neighboring lounger and waited for the Brits to go in the sauna.

They showed no sign of doing any such thing.

Why had the man been standing by Sokolov's lounger? Had he started rummaging through his things only to be interrupted by Allmen? Did he have the same plan as Allmen? Was he after Sokolov's keycard?

He peered toward the two men. Both looked as if they were sleeping. The one on the nearer lounger was lying on his side, his head facing Allmen.

Allmen waited. It wasn't long before he saw the Brit open his eyes for a second then close them straight away.

Now Allmen realized who they were. These were the Brits who had been one step ahead of him all the way. Now they were one step behind.

He waited for Sokolov to emerge from the sauna. He greeted Allmen with surprise and delight and lay down on his lounger. "Let's have that pick-me-up in fifteen minutes," he suggested.

"Or twenty," Allmen said.

After five more minutes' pretend sleep, Allmen heard the two Brits going to the sauna. Fifteen minutes after that, Sokolov was sufficiently rested.

"Wouldn't you prefer to get changed first, and drink the pick-me-up at the bar?" he suggested. "More elegant than sitting in a bathrobe alongside juice-quaffing health nuts."

Sokolov agreed. As they passed his suite, he took his keycard from his bathrobe pocket and opened the door. Allmen was relieved that the card was still there. He had suggested this minor change to the plan simply to ascertain that.

32

They didn't confine themselves to one pick-me-up. Sokolov knocked back a couple of vodkas, then insisted Allmen order a vodka between glasses of champagne too. "You can only toast your friendship with a Russian with vodka."

It was 4:00 p.m. by the time they withdrew to their rooms.

The first thing Allmen did was call home and tell Carlos about the two surveillance teams. "I'd warn him, ideally. But then he'd vanish forever."

Carlos agreed.

"But if I don't warn him, I'll be helping our competitors."

"You have to get ahead of them, Don John."

"How?"

"Search his room. Take his computer."

"That would be very dangerous, Carlos."

"Our job is very dangerous, Don John."

"More dangerous for me than for you," Allmen muttered.

Toward the end of the conversation he brought up Maria Moreno. "Have I understood correctly? You've hired a cleaning lady?"

Carlos was embarrassed now. "You had more or less promised her, Don John."

"Can we afford it?" Allmen asked. He couldn't recall ever having asked that question before.

"Certainly, if we conclude this case successfully," Carlos observed slyly.

Allmen attempted to take the siesta he had missed. But he couldn't sleep. He tried to read, but his mind was going around in circles. Finally he sat by the window and stared out at the sea. That didn't help either. It lay there like an unsolved riddle.

When Allmen got to the dining room that evening, Sokolov was already sitting at his table in the opposite corner. They waved to each other, and each ate alone.

Sokolov's reticence was not wholly inconvenient. Vanessa was in the dining room. She was sitting just a few tables away, giving Allmen occasional furtive glances. If he had been eating with his beach acquaintance yet again, she might have come to the wrong conclusion.

But when Sokolov finished his food and indicated with a gesture that he would wait for him at the bar, Allmen nodded dutifully.

Soon after the Russian, Vanessa and her companion also got up. She looked over at him, and he nodded to them. Only her companion nodded back.

Allmen finished his meal too, and asked the waiter to take his open bottle of Bordeaux to the bar.

It was loud and full there. A luxury liner had dropped anchor and a group of passengers had used their shore leave to drink in a different bar for a change. They were mostly well-heeled, retired couples with tanned faces and coiffured hair.

Sokolov was sitting at the far end of the bar and waved Allmen over. His Bordeaux was already there.

"Thanks for coming," Sokolov said. He smiled and raised his glass to Allmen.

"Just a nightcap," Allmen replied. "I'd like to get an early night."

"That won't be easy," Sokolov noted. "There will be fireworks. In honor of the cruise liner."

They looked out at the ship from their seats. Tall and slender by the side of the long jetty in the sunset. All its windows and portholes were lit, its rigging, railings, and vital contours adorned with garlands of lights.

"Shall we watch the fireworks together? My room has a little bay window looking out at the sea."

The situation was starting to become uncomfortable to Allmen. He recognized the tone of voice, and the way Sokolov was looking at him, from his time at boarding school. This time too he extricated himself politely, without fuss, at the earliest opportunity.

"Pity," Sokolov said. "Such a beautiful evening."

33

It was just before ten when Allmen reached his suite. He called room service and ordered another bottle of the same Bordeaux. He'd left the rest of the last one at the bar.

He dimmed the lights in his salon and sat down at his panorama window.

Now it was night. With its brilliant lights, the ship exuded festivity. Allmen opened one of the French windows. In the distance, music could be heard, a big band playing "In the Mood." He was overcome yet again by the emotion he felt seeing passenger ships: drawn irresistibly aboard. Although he knew that once aboard, he would be drawn irresistibly ashore.

There was a knock. Allmen opened the door to let the room waiter in.

But it was Vanessa.

Standing in front of him in a large hotel robe, looking up with her teasing smile. "Can I come in?"

Allmen let her in.

She walked past him to the window and looked down at the ship. "Have you ever been on a cruise?"

"Many times."

"I've only been once. I found it incredibly boring."

"Me too. Every time."

"Then why did you do it so often?"

"I'm incorrigible."

"Are you still incorrigible?"

"Not in that instance."

Her green eyes scrutinized him. "But in others?"

Allmen nodded.

She put her arms round his neck and kissed him decisively. Suddenly she let go and said, as if she owed him an explanation, "I'm going for a nighttime swim in a minute. I can't go swimming in fine weather; my skin can't handle the sun."

And as if giving him the chance to decide for himself about her skin's sensitivity to sunlight, she opened her bathrobe, slipped it over her shoulders, and let it drop.

Allmen ran his hands down her white body and kissed her.

There was a knock.

Vanessa pushed him away and bent down for her robe.

"Just the room waiter," Allmen whispered.

She kissed her index finger, pressed it to his lips and disappeared into the bedroom.

Allmen opened the door for the waiter, took the wine, and gave him his tip. By the time he'd closed the door and turned round, Vanessa was standing in front of him again. Still naked.

He kissed her again.

And there was another knock.

"Now what?" Allmen shouted crossly.

But it wasn't the room waiter this time.

"It's me, Artyom," a soft voice said.

Vanessa bent down for her robe.

"I'm not free now," Allmen said.

But Vanessa gave him a pat on the backside and said, half wistful, half cheeky, "My husband was right about you two after all."

She opened the door and walked past an aghast Sokolov.

"Have a lovely evening," Allmen heard her add.

Sokolov regained his composure. "Sorry. I'm an asshole. Sorry."

He turned and left. Allmen watched the sad figure till it vanished at the end of the corridor.

He closed the door, opened the bottle, poured himself a glass, sat at the window and looked out at the sea.

Soon he saw a white figure walk onto the beach. She threw off her bathrobe and walked with outspread arms into the sea, swam a few strokes, and emerged again, pulling on her robe, the hood over her head. As she hurried back to the hotel, she rubbed herself dry with the toweling robe.

The night swimmer had ensured her alibi.

Allmen was still awake, the bottle almost empty, when a loud noise broke his thoughts and made him jump. Four jets of light shot into the sky, then dispersed into balls of fire, drizzling a shower of colored light down on the dark surface of the sea.

At the end of the fireworks display the liner expressed its appreciation with three deep notes from its siren. Then he heard the passengers' applause.

Allmen was sad he wasn't one of them.

34

When Allmen entered the breakfast room next morning, neither Sokolov nor Vanessa were among the guests. Nor did they appear during his breakfast.

By the time he'd finished his second macchiato—oh how he missed Gianfranco's lattes at the Viennois—he was the last guest. He signed for his extras and left a suitable tip for the waiter's patience.

At the door, the friendly receptionist approached him. "The time has come, Herr von Allmen. Tomorrow suite 214 will be free. If you're still interested we can do the change-over anytime after 3:00 p.m."

Allmen thanked her. He was looking forward to the bay window, he claimed. He returned to his room, sat at the desk, and considered the situation—he told himself his thinking was more structured sitting at a desk.

If Sokolov really was moving on, he had little chance of staying on his tail. If last night's incident was the reason for Sokolov's sudden change of plan, he could see no chance of deterring him. Allmen was thoroughly straight.

But perhaps Sokolov had other reasons for departing. Perhaps he'd had a message from a contact person. Perhaps the Russian he'd talked to in the pool hadn't just been some fellow countryman he'd met by chance. Perhaps he'd been called to a meeting. Perhaps the diamond had been sold, and the wait for the big money was over. Or had Sokolov simply noticed he was being shadowed and now wanted to escape?

He had to find out what Sokolov was planning. He had to find out where he was going and who he was in contact with.

He had to get into his suite.

Allmen dialed Sokolov's room number. No one answered. He got up, put swimming trunks and bathrobe on, packed his beach basket, and went on the hunt.

It was a pleasant, somewhat windy day. Clouds as white as the hotel floated like swans over the blue sky. Light and shade alternated at a relaxing pace. A super beach day, ideal for people with sensitive skin.

He wasn't on the beach. "Has Herr Sokolov already left, or not yet arrived?" he asked the beach attendant, who had seen him coming and was busy preparing Allmen's chair.

"I'll ask. I've just come on shift."

The beach attendant took his time. When he finally returned, it was in the company of Vanessa and her husband. He took the cover off their chair. And suddenly, as if he'd only just remembered Allmen's question, he called over, "Herr Sokolov hasn't been here yet today."

"Thanks," Allmen murmured.

"No problem!" the beach attendant yelled.

The hint of a sardonic smile hung on Vanessa's lips.

Allmen nodded over to her and continued on his search.

If Sokolov felt anything like he did after that strange night, he was probably hungover. "Sometimes what helps me is the sauna," he had said.

35

The relaxation room was empty. The same meditation music, the same meaningful, shifting colors from the LED lights, the aroma of essential oils.

None of the loungers seemed occupied; there were no towels or bathrobes on any of them.

Allmen went to the corridor leading to the pool area. Before he got there, he met Sokolov coming toward him.

"I ruined your night. I'm sorry. *Izvini.*"

"Forget it."

There was an embarrassed silence.

"Do you want to come in the sauna?" Sokolov asked.

"I'll lie down there. And when you're finished, we can go to the pool bar and rehydrate."

They went to the relaxation room, Sokolov put his things on a lounger, and Allmen settled on the next one.

No sooner had Sokolov disappeared into the sauna than Allmen felt inside the pockets of his bathrobe. In the right one was a phone, in the left the keycard. Allmen took it.

The two Brits were sitting at the pool bar. One was just signing the bill, the other stood next to him, waiting.

If they'd had designs on Sokolov's keycard, they were too late, Allmen thought.

The second-floor corridor was empty except for a cleaning trolley, outside room 198. As he passed, Allmen stole a pair of disposable gloves and stuffed them into his bathrobe pocket.

When he reached 214 he knocked and waited. Nothing.

He knocked again. Still no one came to the door. Allmen put the gloves on and slid the card through the reader. The lock clicked. The door was open.

He switched the "Do Not Disturb" sign from the inside handle to the outside and entered the suite. It was the same as his in reverse. Aside from the bay window in question, the rooms were identical.

The room hadn't yet been made up. The bed was in disarray and there was chaos all around.

Clothes and underwear were strewn across the sheets, undoubtedly flung aside as Sokolov got ready for the sauna. In the bathroom a used towel hung from the faucet of the second basin. The faucet on the other wasn't fully closed.

Through an open wardrobe door he could see the two suits Sokolov had worn in rotation. Two shirts also hung on hangers. On the recamier were shopping bags from a department store in Rostock. Alongside them, three shirts still in their packaging. And four brand new ties, each more hideous than the next.

The safe was in the same cupboard as in his suite, surrounded by both clean and dirty laundry, and the moldy remains of the bowl of fruit the hotel provided each weekend.

Allmen's faint hope that Sokolov had forgotten to lock his safe proved optimistic.

There was nothing hidden among the clothes, nor in the shoes.

Allmen considered where he hid things in hotel rooms himself. His empty luggage occurred to him, the toilet tank, the gaps between sofa and armchair cushions.

Suddenly he heard women's voices from the corridor. They grew louder as they reached the door. Allmen stood stock-still. But then he heard the voices grow quieter again.

He'd been gone fifteen minutes already.

In the bathroom was a toiletries bag, in the side pocket, along with a roll of floss, a small jewelry box.

Allmen's heart missed a beat. He flipped the little lid of the case open. It contained a pair of gold cufflinks with the initials A. S.

He put it back, went into the bedroom, and looked around.

The clothes on the bed! The pants!

In the right pocket was Sokolov's wallet. Alongside receipts, business cards, scraps of paper, and a few hundred euro were three credit cards.

Allmen took them to the safe and slid the magnetic strip on the first card through the reader.

With a soft beep, the lock opened.

The cupboard lights fell on Sokolov's laptop. Allmen took it out. Under it was a bunch of keys, a passport, a small wad of five hundred euro notes, and some car keys.

No diamond. The only pink thing was a small USB flash drive.

Allmen took the flash drive, the laptop, and, given Montgomery's attitude to payment, five of the new, stiff five hundred notes. He locked the safe, returned the credit card to the wallet, the wallet to the pants pocket, opened the door a crack, ensured the coast was clear, and walked to his suite.

He couldn't use his own safe. For that he would have needed a credit card. He placed his haul in a drawer where he kept his own valuables, as he did in all hotels—nothing had ever gone missing—and rushed back to the sauna.

36

The relaxation room had ceased to be relaxing. Spa staff in uniforms were running around with earnest expressions on their faces. Groups of guests in swimsuits and bathrobes stood in clusters talking excitedly in lowered voices.

"What's happened?" Allmen asked a bulky man he'd talked to in the dining room.

"Someone's drowned," he explained, "in the plunge pool. Some people's circulation can't handle the extreme temperature changes."

Allmen walked toward the door to the cool room. A massage therapist who had once massaged him blocked his way. "I'm afraid you're not allowed through here, Herr Allmen."

He looked over her shoulder. Several spa staff were kneeling over a body. Allmen could only see a long, white leg.

"Is that …?"

"I'm afraid so, yes. It's Herr Sokolov."

Allmen was rooted to the spot. He stared over at the group of assistants. And at Sokolov's long, thin leg.

It was only when the ambulance crew and emergency doctor needed to pass him that he regained movement.

Slowly, numbed, he walked toward the exit. By the pool he remembered Sokolov's keycard. He returned and sat down on Sokolov's lounger, as if in shock. He was so convincing the massage therapist soon came over after to ask if everything was okay.

"I'll be alright," Allmen said, and the therapist returned to her post.

As he got up, he slid Sokolov's card back into the bathrobe.

PART 3

37

The rain beat down on the beach chair canopy. The drops made tiny hollows in the fine sand. The flat stones were washed clean and shone like gemstones. From time to time a gull screeched, echoing its own sad cry then letting it die away.

From the spa Allmen had gone straight to his room and tried to call Carlos. Maria Moreno had answered yet again, and informed him that Señor de Leon was busy.

"It is very, very urgent," he insisted impatiently.

"He's over in the villa. A burst pipe. Please try again later."

Allmen opened the drawer that held his valuables. He took the laptop out and looked around the suite.

Over the desk hung an oil painting, a flower study of dubious quality in a heavy gold frame. He pulled it away from the wall slightly, placed the laptop upright within the stretcher on the backside of the frame, and carefully replaced it.

Then he tried to call Carlos again, this time with success.

"Carlos, they've killed Sokolov."

There was silence for a moment. Then Carlos asked, "Who?"

"The Brits, I think. Drowned in the plunge pool at the sauna. I saw them close by just before it happened."

Another short silence before Carlos said, "So they got there before us again."

"Not entirely, Carlos." Allmen told him about the laptop.

"Come home as soon as you can, Don John."

He had only just put the phone down when it rang again. It was reception. They were sorry but suite 214 would not be available just yet after all. The police needed to carry out an investigation first.

That was absolutely fine, Allmen said, and apologized himself as his plans had also changed and he would not now be needing either that suite or his current suite. He asked them to arrange a flight for the next day, to book the limousine and prepare the invoice.

Then he went to the beach.

Only a few days ago he had sat next to Sokolov here. "That's my career goal too," he'd said, when Allmen explained he was a man of leisure. And now, just before achieving it, he had died.

Allmen felt melancholy. And the sense of departure he always felt leaving a hotel wasn't helping. The knowledge that the rooms that had been his home for a few days would soon be occupied by other people was, as ever, a reminder of the transience of existence. The constant coming and going of guests and seasons was what he loved about hotels, and why he always felt wistful on leaving.

The weather had turned. Here and there the afternoon sun slipped through a chink between long clouds the color of the sea, gray splashed with spumes of white. A few of the chairs were occupied. At the beach bar the first guests had sat down.

38

Beyond the washed-up seaweed, yesterday's sandcastles trickled to ruins in the east wind.

Allmen went for one last walk along the beach. His suitcases stood packed in his suite. His anthracite-gray suit was the only thing hanging in the wardrobe. In two hours the limousine would be waiting for him.

Last night the atmosphere in the dining room had been subdued. The guests were either in shock after the fatal accident or felt required out of decency to exercise a certain restraint. At his corner table Allmen felt like a widower, subject to furtive glances and whispers from other guests. Vanessa actually went as far as offering her sympathies.

She got up suddenly from her table, crossed the room, offered her hand, placed the other on his shoulder, and said, "My heartfelt condolences. It must be terrible for you."

Allmen stood up and replied, "I barely knew him really," feeling strangely guilty about this posthumous distancing.

Afterward she returned to her table. Judging by his facial expression, her husband had said something unfriendly. She put her cutlery down; he continued eating.

After supper Allmen had drunk a couple of vodkas with the barman in Sokolov's memory, then gone to his room to start packing.

Now the hotel was full of police officers, questioning the guests. Allmen's first impulse was to approach them and tell them about the Brits. But then he changed his mind. He didn't want to draw unnecessary attention to himself. If he were asked, he would mention them. If not, he would try to leave discreetly.

Now he had left the hotel's private beach and entered the public stretch. The beach chairs here were colorful and individualistic, like the huts in a colony of dachas.

A voice behind him called out, "Herr von Allmen, excuse me." It sounded out of breath.

Allmen turned. The voice belonged to a young, slightly overweight man with short blond hair. He held up a police ID and offered his hand.

"Krille. We heard you are leaving and wanted to ask a few questions," he explained. "Otherwise I wouldn't interrupt your stroll on the beach. Shall we walk on?"

They continued walking together.

"You were a friend of Herr Sokolov?"

"We ate together twice, had a drink at the bar once, and visited the spa together once," Allmen corrected him.

"Nothing more?"

Allmen stopped and looked at Krille. It wasn't hard to guess what was meant by his question.

"Whatever anyone has told you, I did not have a relationship with Sokolov. Not with him or with any man ever."

Krille took this on board without comment. "What were you doing at the time of the … er … incident in the sauna."

"The relaxation room is perfect for reading and resting. You don't get disturbed by noisy children."

Krille scribbled something in his tiny notebook. Allmen surprised him with a question: "Are you working on the assumption this was an accident?"

The officer scrutinized him. "Did you notice anything that might suggest otherwise?"

Allmen described both his sightings of the Brits, that they had followed Sokolov from the beach. That he had surprised one of them prowling around Sokolov's lounger.

"Would you be prepared to make a statement to that effect?"

"If it doesn't cause me to miss my flight."

Krille halted. "Then we'd better head back. You will be picked up in under two hours."

The man had been informed in detail about Allmen's plans.

They walked past the randomly arrayed beach chairs back to the orderly ones.

"We inquired which of the guests were leaving ahead of schedule. You were the only one. Apart from the two British men. They checked out yesterday."

Allmen stopped still. "I saw one of them in the relaxation room after it happened. There were several witnesses."

Krille nodded. "I know."

Allmen braced himself for the sentence, *you were there more than once, however*. What the investigator said instead was not much better: "Do you know anything about the laptop?"

"The laptop?"

"Sokolov was often seen with a laptop. We haven't found it yet."

An intuition made Allmen reply, "That's strange; Herr Sokolov always had it on him."

"Even in the sauna?"

Allmen shook his head. "In the relaxation room. On the occasion I was with him there, when he went into the sauna he left the laptop in the relaxation room."

"Just lying around?"

"No, in his beach bag, covered by a bathrobe."

"So someone could have stolen the laptop in the relaxation room."

"Easily. Why is it so important?"

"Because it's gone."

Allmen looked at him in surprise. "Yes, of course."

"One more question, Herr von Allmen. Where were you before you went to the sauna?"

"On the beach."

"And you went straight from there to the sauna?"

"Straight there. There are witnesses to that."

The investigator nodded. "Indeed."

"Why do you ask then?"

"Just procedure. Someone searched Sokolov's room."

Anyone leading a life like Allmen's learns not to let their face go red or white. This time too he succeeded.

"*Searched* doesn't quite do it justice," Krille observed. "Turned it upside down." And after a few steps he added.

"Broke in and ransacked it, in extreme haste."

Allmen succeeded in hiding his relief.

They had almost reached the hotel. "One final request," Krille said. "This is a little unorthodox, but given the tight timeframe …"

"Ask away."

"We don't have a search warrant, but in this case it would be granted within a few hours. Would you mind if my colleague took a quick look in your luggage *before* we get the paperwork, while we record your statement? Otherwise your departure might be delayed."

Again, Allmen's experience of delicate situations stood him in good stead. "Just be quick about it," was his only comment.

The investigator called a colleague and sent him to Allmen's suite. Then they walked to the hotel in silence.

39

With all the calm he could muster Allmen sat in the armchair by the window and gave his statement while Krille typed it into his laptop and another officer searched his luggage. This consisted of a matching set, now rather worn, which he'd had made in better times at the Louis Vuitton workshop in Asnières, in neutral black, not with Louis Vuitton's initials but with J. F. v. A.

As the officer began searching, he said, "Please do it in a way that I can still get the suitcases shut. I don't have time to repack."

The man took a lot of care, he had to admit. Disdainful but impressed, his expression suggested he had never handled luggage like this. Everything had its place. The toiletries were in the toiletries box, the ties in the tie case, the shirts in the shirt carrier; everything detachable and fitting neatly together. Even the dirty laundry had its own bag, of soft leather.

For shoes there was a separate, flat case and for the suits a large one, which folded out into a little wardrobe.

At one point the officer said, "But you can't check all this in."

"Why not?" Allmen asked, perplexed.

"It would cost a fortune in excess baggage."

"Oh, I see. Well, yes."

The final piece was a little larger than a briefcase—Allmen's entertainment case, with space for around twenty books, two Bluetooth speakers, and an iPod loaded with operas, symphonies, rock, folk, and jazz—depending on his mood.

The officer carefully emptied the case. As he began refilling it, he noticed two loops on the bottom, left and right.

"Does this open?"

Allmen nodded.

The man pulled the loops, the base opened up and revealed—a backgammon board. A separate case held the pieces, and in another were playing cards for bridge, poker, skat, and jass.

Allmen helped him close the cases and the officer took a last look in the wardrobes and drawers.

"If you would excuse me for a moment. I just have to change."

Krille thanked Allmen for his patience and understanding, and the two men said goodbye. Allmen changed into his suit and packed the clothes he'd been wearing.

Then he cautiously removed the flower painting above the desk from the wall and retrieved the laptop. He took the backgammon board from the base of the entertainment case, unfolded it, hid the little computer in the hollow space inside, and stowed it back in the base of the bag.

He informed the reception desk that his luggage was ready to be collected and went downstairs to the lobby.

The charming receptionist was on duty. He slid one of Sokolov's five hundred notes over the desk toward her and thanked her for taking good care of him.

He skimmed the invoice—with all the extras, it came to somewhere over fourteen thousand euro—and signed it.

"You have my address," he said casually, and shook the receptionist's hand. "Ah, and while I think of it: address the letter to F. A. O. Herr Carlos de Leon, my personal assistant. Otherwise it may go astray."

The chauffeur drove the Bentley faster this time as they were running late.

But the hotel had informed the airport. The check-in desk was kept open longer for Herr von Allmen.

40

Saturday was a good day to come home. Carlos had the whole day off and could give him a decent welcome.

While Herr Arnold unpacked the luggage from the trunk of the Cadillac, Allmen pressed the bell beneath the brass plaque with his initials.

Shortly afterward, Carlos appeared with a handcart dating back to the villa's first owner.

"Muy buenas tardes," he wished his *patrón,* *"bienvenido."* He loaded up the luggage.

Meanwhile Allmen remunerated Herr Arnold appropriately.

Carlos went ahead down the flagstone path, the cart rattling, till just before the carved wooden door to the villa, then turned left around the box tree and wound his way through the rhododendrons and azaleas to the tiny gardener's cottage.

It was high summer, late afternoon, and the mature species trees offered a cool, pleasant shade. Carlos had made tea, which he served in the library, along with his inimitable nachos with guacamole and frijoles. While Allmen drank some tea, Carlos unpacked the cases.

Then he returned to the library, poured more tea, and waited, as ever, for Allmen's invitation to join him. Only then did he sit down.

"You found the laptop, right?"

"Yes, Don John." He laughed. "Good hiding place."

Allmen invited Carlos to help himself to the snacks. Carlos thanked him and took one.

"I told the police about the Brits," Allmen said. "They left that same day."

"And about the Americans?"

"I said nothing about them."

Carlos didn't ask why. Instead he revealed some surprising news. "Señor Montgomery transferred the money yesterday."

Allmen acted as if he had expected no different.

"And he left a message. You are to call him urgently."

Carlos passed him a telephone memo with Montgomery's number and the time of the call. It wasn't Carlos's handwriting. Allmen looked inquiringly at him.

"Señorita Moreno. She took the call."

"Have you hired her full time now?" Allmen was amused by Carlos's awkwardness.

"No, no. But she is very efficient. A great help."

"I see."

Carlos cleared his throat. "Don John?"

"Diga!"

"When you talk to Montgomery, do you plan to mention the laptop?"

Allmen shook his head.

"*Muy bien*, Don John." Carlos stood up. "If we have nothing else to discuss, then I'll examine it."

"Yes please, go ahead."

"Could you write 'pink diamond' in Russian for me?" Carlos handed him a piece of paper. Allmen took his fountain pen and wrote the two words in Cyrillic script. Then Carlos left him alone.

Allmen called Montgomery's number. He answered instantly. Allmen informed him about Sokolov's death. Montgomery's response was businesslike. He didn't wish to know any details and didn't ask about the circumstances. It was as if all he was hearing was the official confirmation of information he had known for some while. Allmen's suspicion that the two Brits were Montgomery's men was lent further credence.

"We're on target," he said simply.

"Could you be a tad more specific?" Montgomery sounded cross.

"Not on the telephone."

"Then in person, in London. When?"

Allmen proposed waiting till tomorrow to see how the investigation had progressed, then coming up with some possible meeting times. Montgomery agreed and hung up.

Allmen put the memo with the phone number in the outside pocket of his suit. There he found the pink flash drive from Sokolov's safe. He put it in one of the many drawers in his bureau, sat down at the piano, and relaxed with a little Cole Porter.

41

Meanwhile Carlos was sitting at the little desk in his garret with Sokolov's laptop.

A wonderful device, no comparison with his old thing. The tiny computer was crammed with software. Mostly programs Carlos had only heard of, at best, special tools for programmers. But there were also lots of useful things, out of Carlos's price range, for image manipulation, design, text, music, and so on.

Carlos began searching the hard disk.

The calendar was empty. Either wiped or never used. The address book contained 130 addresses in Cyrillic script.

Carlos searched for the word "pink" in English, German, and Russian, in vain. There were no results for "diamond" in any of the languages either.

Sokolov's inbox didn't seem to have been emptied for years. Carlos found messages going back to 2007. Most were in Cyrillic script. But there were a few German and English ones. Carlos had picked up English from the tourists as a little shoeshine boy. He had spoken German ever since living in Switzerland. So he could easily have read and understood the messages if they hadn't been technical discussions, which most were. They were full of expressions that meant nothing to him.

Here too, there were no hits in the search for "pink diamond" in the three languages.

He had no choice then but to open each email individually and read the German and English ones. For the last eight months alone there were nearly three thousand received and sent messages. Most of the English ones were about business. Sokolov rarely mixed his work with his private life. He had had one extremely private relationship with a certain Günther, with whom he had corresponded in very racy German. The only business relationship that was also personal was with someone from New York called Paul La Route. One of the emails referred to an evening in which they had clearly had a lot to drink. Another included a photo of the villa in Spätbergstrasse and an invitation to La Route to come there when he was next in Zurich.

Carlos worked back as far as April. Then he switched the laptop off. He packed it in two plastic bags, secured them with wide packing tape, attached a long rope to the package, and took it to his bedroom, where the attic window faced away from the villa. It was night now. Carlos climbed out onto the roof. Even as a boy he had earned a bit of money from the gringos climbing high into the crowns of their trees with a machete to prune them and free them of mistletoe. He had no fear of heights.

He climbed up the snow guards to the chimney, pushed the package inside, and let it down a few yards. He tied the string and climbed back down to his bedroom window.

Allmen had stopped playing the piano, but Carlos could still hear him puttering around. He went downstairs and gave him the bad news that he had found nothing.

42

Viennois was almost empty. Several of the habitués were on vacation and the tourists, who at this time of year typically competed with the remaining 10:00 a.m. guests for their regular tables, were sitting at the tables outside. It was a lovely summer's day.

Allmen's mood was low. Sokolov's death had really sunk in. The suspicion that his client Montgomery was involved unnerved him, and Viennois reminded him of another worry, the mysterious American who looked like Martin Sheen.

Gianfranco brought his second coffee and a croissant. Shaking his head he exclaimed, *"Quarantacinque milioni per un anello, Signor Conte!"* Forty-five million for a ring, Count Allmen!

Allmen looked at him in surprise. Gianfranco pointed to an article in the newspaper in front of his guest. Allmen hadn't noticed it yet.

The piece took up a quarter of a page. The headline read, "The Pink Diamond Comes Out." Beneath it was a smiling Asian lady wearing a red bridal dress. She was holding up her left hand, on which she wore a large solitaire.

"Li Hua Jiao, daughter of major Chinese investor Zhang Wei Linh, and her wedding present," the caption read.

The article explained that the buyer of the pink diamond, which had achieved the record price of over forty-five million francs at Murphy's Swiss auction house, had only remained anonymous because he wished to surprise his daughter with it at her wedding. He was the Chinese multi-millionaire Zhang Wei Linh, whose daughter Hua Jiao had married the Chinese pop star Li Feng Hu last weekend.

43

Carlos was wearing his waiter's jacket with black trousers and a tie, something he rarely did on weekdays, with such a short lunch break. But when Allmen caught the smell of coq au vin—one of his favorite dishes—he realized Carlos had found out.

He went to the library and sat in his reading chair. Carlos served him a sherry.

Allmen drank half the glass and looked at him, baffled. "Can you comprehend it?"

Carlos shook his head.

"Why would he hire us to look for something that never disappeared?"

"Perhaps the diamond did disappear, but someone else found it."

"Do you believe that?"

"I'm not sure, Don John."

Allmen finished his sherry and, atypically, requested a second. Carlos poured it.

Allmen took it and pondered. "The bride was wearing

the diamond on her finger the day after Sokolov died. Perhaps they got Sokolov to talk before they drowned him."

Carlos repeated, "I'm not sure, Don John." He excused himself; the food would be ready in a moment.

Allmen took his sherry, went to the cramped, over-furnished living-dining room, and sat at the table, set for a special occasion.

Carlos brought in the salad, grown by him on the tiny vegetable plot in the less shady area of the garden. The various salad leaves were drizzled with a lemon, macadamia oil, and herb dressing, layered into a little mound, and decorated with tomatoes steeped in olive oil.

Allmen made no comment on the tiny work of art. Instead he said, "When I talked to Montgomery on Saturday, the bride already had the pink diamond."

"She probably did, Don John."

Allmen ate, not paying the food the attention it deserved.

"Why didn't he tell me that? Do you have any explanation, Carlos?"

"Two possibilities, Don John. Either the diamond never disappeared. Or Montgomery didn't know it had been found because the two Brits were working for the Chinese."

"And what would Montgomery's role have been then?"

"Maybe he was used. Like us, Don John."

Carlos cleared the plate and brought the main course. The chicken flesh was dark red and falling from the bones. The polenta was drenched in a thick wine sauce with diced bacon and pearl onions swimming in it. And yet Allmen had to force himself to finish his plate.

"Carlos?" Allmen asked, when he looked in for the third time to see if he could clear the table.

"*Qué manda*, Don John?"

"Did Sokolov have nothing to do with the pink diamond then?"

"I think he did, Don John."

"Yes?"

Carlos nodded. "But the pink diamond is not what we think it is."

44

Allmen tried time after time to get Montgomery on the phone until, soon after ten, he gave up. He put Brahms's *Variations on a Theme by Haydn* on, with Harnoncourt and the Berlin Philharmonic, and attempted to read.

A sudden smashing of glass, loud like an explosion. Allmen leaped out of the chair but was grabbed from behind. A hand stifled him and everything went black.

A sharp pain shot through his left and then his right arm. He was pushed roughly onto the chair.

The next thing he knew he was sitting, breathing heavily, in his reading chair. His arms were tied tightly behind his back, shoulders, elbows, and wrists a mass of pain.

Now he heard noises from the vestibule, the sound of a scuffle.

"*Hijo de puta!*" Carlos's voice cried.

An Englishman's voice: "Jack! Over here!"

The man standing behind Allmen ran off. Now he saw him for the first time: black t-shirt, jeans, black stocking over his head. He vanished through the door to the living-dining room, knocking something over. It sounded like the little house bar.

The noise of fighting continued. Carlos again, with *"Hijos de puta!"* A blow that sounded like a fist on a sandbag, then silence, just the sound of panting.

Two men entered the library, holding Carlos by his arms and legs like a slain deer. They dropped him on the kilim rug, just within Allmen's field of view. Carlos's eyes and mouth were half open and he was bleeding from his nose.

One of the two crouched in front of Allmen and looked at him. He was dressed in black too, but his stocking was brown. His right eye was swollen half shut. Most likely Carlos's work.

He opened his hand. "You give it to me, and we'll be gone." He spoke with a London accent.

"What?" Allmen spluttered.

"What Sokolov had. And you've got now. It doesn't belong to either of you."

Carlos groaned. The other man kicked him.

"Can't you see what pain he's in!" Allmen shouted at him.

The man gave Carlos another kick.

The first man held his hand out, more demanding.

"I don't know what you're talking about."

Carlos received another kick.

"Stop that!"

Another kick.

Allmen had lost all feeling in his hands and could feel the numbness creeping up his arms. Carlos was bleeding and had stopped groaning, which Allmen took as a bad sign. He gave up. He pointed to the bureau with his chin. "There. In one of the drawers."

Carlos groaned loudly, and received another kick.

The Londoner walked toward the bureau. "Which one?"

Allmen sighed. "I can't remember."

The man pulled out the first of the tiny veneered drawers, tipped it out onto the desktop, and sifted through the contents. The other man joined him to help.

Behind the two, Allmen suddenly saw two other men emerge from the next room. They were holding pistols and signaled for him to keep quiet.

Another drawer was turned out.

"Freeze!" one of the armed men said. Then, "Down!"

In a few seconds the two Londoners were lying handcuffed on their stomachs. Each move was perfect, as if all four had choreographed the arrest.

45

As soon as the two Brits were lying, tied up, on their stomachs, Carlos pulled himself to his feet. He was wearing a pair of Allmen's old pajamas, altered to fit him, and wiped the blood from his nose with the sleeve. He went over to the man with the black stocking and gave him a kick. *"Uno,"* he counted. And then four more: *"Dos, tres, cuatro, cinco.* Five times, *hijo de puta."*

One of their rescuers was talking quietly on the telephone, the other helped Allmen out of the armchair and cut the cable ties he was bound with.

Allmen lifted his numbed hands and looked at his wrists. The plastic had cut deep. In a few places his skin was broken and bleeding.

"Are you alright?" the first rescuer asked. Clearly an American.

"I'm fine," Allmen stated. He wanted to take his dress handkerchief from his breast pocket to offer to Carlos, but he was having trouble controlling his hands.

Carlos saw what he intended and deterred him with a wave. Ultimately he was the one responsible for washing and ironing. He left the library. He returned right away holding a bundle of paper towels to his nose.

Now the Americans had turned the intruders on their backs and removed their masks.

They were the two Brits from the Grand Duc.

The other rescuer had finished his telephone conversation and returned to the library. It was the man who resembled Martin Sheen. He offered his hand.

Allmen attempted to shake it, without success. "No feeling," he explained.

The American took Allmen's limp hand and shook it. "Bob," he introduced himself. "And this is Joey."

"Hi!" his partner called, without letting the two Brits out of his sight.

Allmen introduced Carlos, still standing with his head tipped back and paper towel against his nose.

"Are you alright?" Bob now asked Carlos.

He answered with a brave, *"Sí, señor."*

"Thank you for the assistance. How did you know what was going on here?" Allmen asked.

"We have been—how can I put it?—protecting you."

"On whose behalf?"

"On behalf of someone who owns something that you have."

"The same thing these two wanted?" Allmen pointed to the bound men.

"Same thing."

"And who are they working for?"

"The competition." Bob's cellphone rang. He answered,

said "Okay," and ended the call. "They're here," he said briefly to the other man. He nodded and left.

Bob went over to the bureau and began searching.

"And what is this thing everyone wants?" Allmen asked.

"This." Bob had found Sokolov's pink flash drive and held it up.

The other American returned, accompanied by three men. They greeted Bob like a friend and nodded swiftly to Allmen and Carlos. Two of them helped the Brits to their feet and led them away.

The third briefly held an official-looking ID under Allmen's nose and said in Swiss German, "We'll be in contact." He said goodbye and followed his colleagues.

Allmen looked at Bob. "Who were they?"

"*Your* federal police. How did you come into possession of this?" Bob held out the flash drive.

Allmen improvised. "Sokolov gave it to me. I was supposed to look after it for him."

"And what about his laptop?"

"I thought the two Brits had stolen it."

"That's what the German police think too." The American put the storage device in his pants pocket and started to leave.

"One more question, Bob," Allmen said. "How did you find your way to the Grand Duc?"

"We were tailing the Brits."

"And how did they find their way there?"

"They were tailing you."

"But why were you in Café Viennois that time?"

"Because the Brits were there."

As Bob said goodbye, the feeling returned to Allmen's hands again. And with it the pain of the incisions.

Carlos's nose had stopped bleeding and he accompanied the Americans to the door. He returned with a brush and pan and started sweeping up the broken glass.

"Do you know how the Brits found us, Carlos?"

"*Sí*, Don John: Señor Montgomery."

"And what do you think is on the little flash drive?"

"I don't know, Don John. But that is the pink diamond."

46

Despite the warm weather, Allmen felt forced to hide the marks from the cable ties under heavy double cuffs. Even at these temperatures, he never committed the sartorial sin of wearing short sleeves under a jacket. But he did resort normally to light summer shirts with simple cuffs and plain mother-of-pearl buttons.

For Carlos it was even harder. The evidence of the fight was on his face. Glowing in a spectrum of colors, his eye was so conspicuous he didn't dare go out on the street. An illegal immigrant needed to be as unobtrusive as possible.

The problem was groceries. For the first time in his life, Carlos did the unthinkable. He asked his *patrón* to go shopping. He gave him a neat, clear shopping list, including a few everyday supplies: bread, cheese, butter, cream, beef cubes, a spring chicken, paper towels, and toilet paper. He wrote the name of the supermarket down, and sketched out where to find the various products.

Allmen remained unequal to the challenge. He failed to grasp the system for releasing the shopping carts, and once he'd learned it by watching a housewife, he found he didn't have the requisite two-franc coin. He made do with a basket and set out on the hunt.

The first thing he found was the most embarrassing item, toilet paper. He noted the location, intending to return when he had a few more products as camouflage.

It took him a quarter of an hour to find them again. He took two rolls—the large family packs were too conspicuous—and covered them with the six frozen pizzas he had decided on instead of the items listed. He could eat out and Carlos could eat the pizzas, practical and less work, till he felt ready for the outside world again.

Allmen went to the checkout and paid in cash, amazed at how cheap it was. He nearly gave the cashier a tip out of habit.

In the supermarket parking lot Herr Arnold was waiting with the Cadillac, and stowed the incriminating purchases in the trunk.

Carlos took the groceries from him, stony faced. When Allmen began extolling the virtues of the ready-made pizzas, he answered with his *"Cómo no, cómo no."* Then he went to the kitchen and stuffed the pizzas into the freezer.

The next time Allmen saw him was at teatime. He poured the tea in silence.

"I'm sorry, Carlos, I'm not made for all this domestic business. Why don't you ask Maria Moreno to come and help more often till you're back on your feet?"

"Because we can't afford it, Don John. I don't think we can expect any more money from Señor Montgomery."

"We still have a little left. And there are bound to be some new jobs."

47

But in the days that followed, no new jobs came. Late August granted them a last few fine days. Carlos's beat-up face regained its familiar firm contours. And Allmen returned to his familiar rhythm, alternating between Viennois, siesta, Promenade, the Golden Bar, and the opera.

But in early September two atypical events occurred.

The first was a surprising encounter at the gardener's cottage. Allmen, never an early bird but sometimes a nighthawk, came home shortly before six in the morning. After his dinner at Promenade he'd looked in at Süden, a new club whose recent opening he'd been taken to by a friendly drinking companion, and whose promoter had been so impressed by his manner and appearance he'd pressed a VIP card on him.

He'd had a drink, and another, both on the house, and just as he'd wanted to leave, he was detained by the arrival of Jasmin, a friend from the good times, and swept back to the bar. Later he accompanied her home and accepted her invitation for a good-night beer.

It was a brisk morning. There was dew on the lawn and a hint of fall in the air. Allmen was walking toward the gardener's cottage, keyring in hand, when he saw two figures detaching themselves from each other at the half-open front door. The man was Carlos, the woman—Maria Moreno.

The two gentlemen were somewhat more embarrassed than the lady. She greeted Allmen unself-consciously, and after a few pleasantries, let Carlos accompany her to the garden gate.

The second significant occurrence was the visit by an officer of the Swiss federal police, a man in his mid-fifties, very polite and formal, with a very small notebook that he balanced on his knee while deftly taking down Allmen's statement.

When he'd finished, Allmen asked, "Those two drowned Sokolov, didn't they?"

The officer nodded.

"Do we know why?"

"They're saying it was an accident. They were trying to get information from him by repeatedly pushing him under the water. He drowned in the process."

"And you believe that?"

"Herr Sokolov must have fought very hard. He was covered in bruises and had traces under his fingernails matching that pair's DNA."

"What will happen to them?"

"They've been left in the hands of our German colleagues."

"Do we know who they were working for?"

"We are working on a particular, specific assumption. I can't say any more at this stage of the investigation."

"A certain Herr Montgomery?"

The officer remained silent.

"And do we know who Montgomery was working for?"

The officer got up, handed Allmen his card and said, "If anything else occurs to you, please get in touch."

Otherwise the days passed peacefully and without incident. Allmen International Inquiries shelved the pink diamond case. Allmen put all his creative energies back into feigning solvency. And Carlos began to worry about his decision to halve his hours for K, C, L & D Trust Company, worries that the fun-loving, optimistic Maria Moreno knew how to banish.

48

Since acquiring some savings, thanks to the commission on the dragonflies, Carlos had begun to take an interest in financial issues. And this was how he came to read the following article in the business section of a weekly newspaper Allmen had read and discarded:

Hedge & Win under Investigation

The British hedge fund Hedge & Win may be behind the theft of the HFT software that a former employee of investment bank Brookfield Klein was carrying when arrested at Boston's Logan International Airport, according to a statement from the New York District Attorney's office, which is investigating the case.

The computer program is the result of many years' work. The bank uses it to carry out high-frequency transactions. During the months prior to his arrest, the suspect, a Canadian named Paul La Route, former employee of Brookfield Klein, was in constant communication with the hedge fund.

Paul La Route? The name sounded familiar.

It was getting dark earlier now, and the moon was nearly new, so Carlos was able to climb the chimney without fear of being seen.

It was still mild and there was no wind. The villa stood in darkness; through the windows he saw the faint lights and flashing LEDs of office equipment. The large glass roof of the library was dimly lit. From the baby grand came the sound of the nocturne that Allmen played decently.

Carlos lifted the laptop carefully out of the chimney and climbed back down to his attic window.

There were thirteen emails to and from La Route. The first went, "Hi Artyom, back in NYC, still hungover but sober enough to make one thing clear—I meant it about the Vivid P project. I hope you did too. Cheers! Paul."

The reply was from the same day: "Hi Paul, let's go then! Artyom."

La Route had answered straight back: "Great! You'll be hearing from me. Paul."

After ten days' radio silence came the next message. It contained a link to a server and the information, "user: artyom, password: vividp33," and the instructions to download the file before 5:00 p.m. New York time, save it straight to a flash drive then delete it from the hard disk. La Route would then delete it from the server.

By 10:00 a.m. Swiss time the confirmation from Sokolov had already come: "Copied and deleted."

A minute later the confirmation from La Route: "deleted."

A few days later Sokolov wrote to La Route: "X highly interested! Negotiate?"

La Route replied, "Negotiate."

Then came five more emails on the subject. The first announced a bank transfer—"your share of the advance payment"—to the tune of two hundred thousand dollars, and the request for bank details.

An email including Sokolov's bank details was sent an hour later.

It was then three weeks till there was another message, with the subject line "vivid p." It was from Sokolov to La Route and went, "Hi Paul, next time you visit you can stay with me—check the photo. Regards, Artyom." Attached was a photo of a detached house, which Carlos recognized as the villa on Spätbergstrasse.

But then, a few days later, there was a message in Sokolov's inbox flagged extremely urgent. Headed "Troubles!!!" it read, "Make backup copy, hide in very safe place—tell me where. Wipe everything that might connect us! Everything!"

Sokolov's answer was dated the same day. It consisted of a single word: "Grotto."

Carlos did searches for the term "vivid p," for messages to and from "Paul," repeated the procedure with "La Route," searched the contents of all the emails in all the folders for the most important words used in these thirteen mails—nothing. No further clue about the pink diamond.

Piano chords were still drifting up. Carlos shut the laptop, put it under his arm, and descended the narrow, steep steps.

49

Allmen's thoughts would also have been revolving around the conundrum of the pink diamond, if he hadn't distracted himself with the nocturne. Not every kind of piano playing worked as a distraction. If he just bashed out something from his repertoire his thoughts soon wandered from the music and, before he knew it, ended up back in the place he'd tried to lure them from. But when he played from sheet music he needed all his brainpower. This didn't do much for his playing, but it was the most effective thing apart from reading for escaping reality.

When Carlos dragged him back to the latter with his *"Con permiso,"* Allmen started.

"Disculpe," Carlos said. "I could hear you were still awake."

"What did you want?"

"It's about the pink diamond."

Allmen spread the cover over the piano keys, closed the lid, and got up.

Carlos showed him the newspaper article. Allmen offered him a seat on the art deco suite, sat down himself, and read the piece.

"And now you think our little flash thing was this program?"

"I don't think; I know." Carlos flipped the laptop open and placed it on the coffee table. He opened the first mail. *"Fíjese,* Don John! Can you imagine it! The message is from Paul La Route to Artyom Sokolov."

"No me diga!" Allmen exclaimed, and started to read.

By the second email, it was clear to Allmen that Sokolov was La Route's accomplice.

"Vivid P," Allmen said. "You know what that means? Vivid pink—the technical term for a pink diamond!"

At the third email, a message appeared on the screen asking them to plug the computer into the outlet; the battery was almost empty.

"Look," Allmen said, pointing to the screen.

"I don't have a power cord."

"Why not?"

"Because—with all due respect, Don John—you didn't steal it. I've ordered one. It will probably arrive tomorrow."

Allmen vaguely remembered seeing a cable in the chaos of Sokolov's room. He read on.

"Mission completed. Program copied and wiped," was his comment on the fifth email.

At the seventh he looked at Carlos, who nodded. *"Fíjese!* La Route sold it to Hedge&Win while Sokolov negotiated with other interested parties!"

Then he was silent till the ninth. "Two hundred thousand dollars advance! What was the total? It must have been a lot! He said he was practicing being wealthy until the wealth arrived."

The photograph in the eleventh mail caused Allmen to comment, "Isn't it hideous, that villa in Spätbergstrasse?"

Carlos said nothing. Villas in that district were so far out of his realm, he had no opinion on their aesthetics. But he responded to Allmen's next comment, on the twelfth email headed "Troubles!!!" in which La Route instructed Sokolov to make a backup copy and wipe all traces of contact between them.

"He must have suspected they were onto him," Allmen surmised.

Carlos had done the research. "Two days later he was arrested at the airport in Boston."

Allmen leant back and thought for a moment. "So a backup copy exists."

Carlos made a vague gesture.

"What makes you think otherwise?"

"I don't think he was very reliable. The email correspondence with Señor La Route, Don John—he didn't actually delete it."

"True. Sokolov was slovenly. You should have seen his room."

They both fell silent.

Then suddenly they realized. "The Brits," Allmen said. "The Brits were working for Hedge&Win."

"Because Señor La Route, to whom they'd already paid a lot of money, had been arrested before he could hand over the software," Carlos continued.

"They were tracking Sokolov, and knew he had a copy of

the software he was planning to sell to third parties through his connections in the IT business."

"That means, Don John, that Montgomery was working for Hedge&Win. He set those two onto you."

"But there's still the question of why he hired Allmen International. Why didn't he set his people straight onto Sokolov?"

"It's easier to carry out investigations in Switzerland if you're Swiss yourself, Don John."

Allmen could see that, but one last question bothered him. "Why Allmen International in particular?"

Carlos smiled. "The website, Don John, the website."

The screen went dark.

"And now what?" Allmen cried out.

"The battery is dead. But there was only one more message. Very short."

"What did it say?"

"Grotto."

"What's that supposed to mean?"

"*Cueva*, cave."

"I understand the word. But what does it mean?"

50

Half past four was early for the Golden Bar. Only three or four tables were occupied. Two men having a discreet business meeting, two ladies enjoying an early aperitif, a young man with a wireless headphone in one ear who seemed to be talking to himself. And Allmen, with Roland Kerbel.

Kerbel was an old friend from the days of Allmen's legendary parties at Villa Schwarzacker. They had never lost touch, although Kerbel was a banker and knew about Allmen's financial situation. He accepted that he wanted to maintain the façade and played along.

Allmen had invited him to this early aperitif because he had "a few questions about the stock market."

"Since when are you interested in the stock market?" Kerbel asked incredulously.

"I've recently acquired a few investments," Allmen replied casually, "and I don't want to sound completely clueless when I talk to my financial advisor."

The banker, fond of the sound of his own voice, gave Allmen an exhaustive explanation of stock trading, then drained his glass. They were both drinking Campari soda, the drink of choice for an early aperitif.

"One last question. What is high-frequency trading?"

"Not relevant in your case. It's something a few banks and hedge funds do."

"And how does it work?"

Kerbel gave the barman a sign to bring two more drinks, and took a deep breath.

"The stock exchanges allow players who use high-frequency trading to get a glance at purchase orders with price ceilings before any other market players get to see them. Say Allmen International was listed on the stock exchange, the shares cost ten dollars, and a buyer puts in an order for a hundred thousand at a limit of ten dollars and ten cents …"

Allmen smiled at the example used.

"The computer buys a hundred thousand Allmen International shares at the market price of ten dollars, driving the buyer up close to his ten-dollar-ten-cent limit. The computer sells him the order for this inflated price and makes a-hundred-thousand-times-ten-cents profit: ten thousand dollars. In absolutely no time."

"How much time exactly?"

"In no time, really."

The barman brought the fresh Camparis and cleared the empty glasses away.

Kerbel took a sip. "Roughly thirty milliseconds."

"The whole process you just described? It takes thirty thousandths of a second?"

"And it's still too long as far as the banks and hedge funds are concerned. They're working away frantically to halve the time, quarter it. They're putting faster and faster, more expensive computers closer and closer to the stock exchange computers to avoid losing more time than necessary to the network. No effort is too much for them in this billion-dollar business."

The darkened gold surfaces throughout the interior reflected the dimmed spotlights, submerging the bar in the constant midnight glow that so flattered its over-forty crowd.

"Billions," Kerbel repeated. "But although this high-frequency trading business is lucrative, it's also highly dangerous. A program like that could get out of control and cause a financial crash. To this day, no one knows what triggered the last flash crash. Some people suspect it was HFT software. The consequences of it landing in the wrong hands don't bear thinking about!"

Kerbel gave his dire warning time to sink in. "Have you heard about the man who was arrested in the States with HFT software in his luggage?"

"Tell me." Allmen took a sip.

"A former employee of Brookfield Klein. The bank is one of the major high-frequency specialists. And the software is a new product the suspect had helped develop himself. That can only mean one thing: it's faster than their competitors' software. That kind of thing induces greed."

"But who can actually use programs like that?"

"The competitors. There's a limited number. Out of the twenty thousand or so firms involved in Nasdaq, only about two hundred engage in high-frequency trading. But they account for over seventy percent of the shares trading.

That narrows the field of suspects. In this case all eyes are on Hedge&Win. A major player. And by no means squeamish either."

The first after-work guests entered the bar, three young men and a young woman, in business attire. They were talking loudly about their bosses, and lowered their voices slightly when they saw how quiet it was in the bar.

"The temptation facing a programmer specializing in high-frequency trading software is huge," Kerbel continued. "They offer him fifty million and he caves."

That evening Allmen waited impatiently for Carlos. He kept looking out, seeing him from a distance hoeing beds, raking grass, watering pots. He hoped he could catch him when he took his wheelbarrow full of garden waste to the compost.

When Carlos finally returned to the gardener's cottage, Allmen waylaid him in the hall and led him straight to the library, just as he was, in overalls and boots. There he described his conversation with Kerbel, the phenomenon of high-frequency trading and the legendary value of the software.

"More than the real diamond, Carlos. *Fíjese!*"

The greenhouse was shaded entirely by the tall trees, just one square of sunlight on the grass at the front, where the hedge began, which demarcated the property from the street. On the top branch of a cedar a blackbird had already begun its evening song.

"And the best thing, Carlos …"

"*Sí,* Don John?"

"I think I know where we should look."

51

Immolux had its offices on the first floor of a town house in the historic center, with a view of the river as it met the lake.

The night before, Allmen had looked for Assistant Vice President Esteban Schuler's business card and finally found it in the breast pocket of the suit he'd been wearing that day. He got up well before Carlos started work and asked him to book an early appointment with Schuler. The earliest available was 3:30 p.m. An assistant vice president's schedule can fill up terribly quickly.

And Schuler kept him waiting, too. His personal assistant offered Allmen a coffee, which he declined. Nor did he wish for a newspaper. Allmen did not believe in salving the consciences of people who kept him waiting by reading or drinking coffee. Anyone who kept Allmen waiting should see him waiting.

After barely four minutes, Schuler burst in, like a chief surgeon called for a home visit. "Do excuse me for the delay."

Allmen ignored Schuler's request to be excused and launched into his speech unceremoniously. "As mentioned earlier on the telephone, Herr Schuler, I cannot get the villa in Spätbergstrasse out of my head."

"I can completely understand that. It's one of our finest properties. But as I said, we have been unable to contact the tenant, the contract runs till the end of the year, and the rent has been paid until then. All I can do is place you at the top of the list of interested parties. But if the tenant decides to extend the contract he does of course take precedent."

Allmen had been nodding as he listened to the explanation. "I propose the following: I'll raise the rent from—what was it? Seventeen plus service charges?"

"Sixteen," Schuler corrected him.

"From sixteen—whatever—to nineteen. We can draw up a contract for ten years, with the option on a further ten. In close consultation with the Immolux architects, I will carry out the necessary improvements—at a rough guess I'd be investing at least a million over the ten-year period. In return, you give the current tenant notice to quit. There are more than enough reasons—neglect, vacancy … And before the end of the week we sign a preliminary agreement outlining these conditions."

Schuler made a face as if he had offers like this every week. "I can certainly get straight in contact with the joint heirs who own the property. When do you need an answer by?"

"Before you do that, I have just one request."

"What's that?"

"Twenty-four hours."

When Allmen saw Schuler hadn't understood, he added, "In the house. Alone. Can you understand that? I respond to moods, atmospheres, vibrations—call it what you will. Even in the most beautiful places, I can't hold out more than an hour if the atmosphere is wrong. Allow me twenty-four hours at 19 Spätbergstrasse and if the atmosphere is right, we'll nail the deal."

Schuler answered in a flash. "That's not possible. Suppose the tenant returned and met you in his house?"

Allmen looked at him defiantly. "Ten thousand francs for your trouble—cash in hand—if he comes back."

Schuler pretended he was still deliberating. "Twenty-four hours? Just yourself?"

"Just myself. And my butler of course." Allmen smiled apologetically. "You know how it is. One feels stranded without him."

52

The house smelled stuffy and damp. The furniture in the hall, still in boxes, gave off a smell of cardboard, wood, and warehouses.

Dust had gathered in the corners of the room. Spiderwebs hung from the heaters and window frames. Dead flies lay on the windowsills. And the evening sun, occasionally breaking through the storm clouds, lit the whitish film coating the windowpanes.

In the large salon, the sofa still stood like a look-out bench in front of the window. Allmen shuddered at the thought that the man who had once sat there was now dead.

There was a sense of death throughout the house. Not just to Allmen, who had known its inhabitant. Also to Carlos.

"Huele la muerte," he said. It smells of death.

Allmen walked straight to the veranda door and unlocked it. As he opened it, a gust of wind blew it almost out of his hand.

The lawn had become a meadow, the grass knee-high. The water in the swimming pool was cloudy. Insects played on its surface. Leaves were rotting on the bottom.

The wind soon rose to a storm, driving dark clouds in from the lake.

In the grotto there was some shelter from the wind.

Moss had spread over the concrete bench that ran along the wall and was creeping along the gaps between the flowery tiles on the ground. The mortar that formed the lumps, dips, and niches of the interior walls was crumbling in several places, leaving dark patches in the once-bright rendering.

The smell of mildew gave the artificiality a more natural feel.

The barbeque was built into a niche beneath the flue. Under it was an unused gas canister, still sealed. The connection tube lay alongside it. The grill was covered by a chrome hood. Allmen lifted it. It folded backward, creaking. An animal ran for cover under the gas burners. Whether a mouse or a lizard, Allmen couldn't be sure.

He opened the fridge, set into the wall close to the barbeque. It must have been switched off, with the door shut, for a long time. He was hit by the stink. Allmen held his nose and looked inside. It was empty aside from a half-full bottle of beer, its label illegible under a layer of mold. He shut the door.

Decorations had been attached to the walls at various points, ornaments made of shells that looked like a child's vacation spoils. In some places they were arranged into sorry garlands and hearts, some formed the frames for sayings or pictures; a few were still intact, painted straight onto the plaster and depicting grapes, oranges, fish, seafood, and Chianti bottles. But mostly they were photographs made unrecognizable by the light and humidity. The shadows of portraits, group photos, and snapshots could just be made out.

They began searching systematically. The gas barbeque was the most complicated. They had to take it apart completely. It was full of cavities, indentations, and hidden recesses. Added to that, the stormy weather meant dusk was beginning early and they were forced to work in dwindling light.

The fridge was full of hiding places too, above all at the back. They pulled it out from its niche in a combined effort and examined the jumble of bars, grids, radiators and wires. Nothing.

Suddenly the storm broke. The lightning and thunder were almost simultaneous, as if the grotto had been struck. The rain beat down as if from a water cannon.

They searched on, undeterred. Although there were lights and light switches in the grotto, there was no power. They were increasingly forced to rely on their sense of touch. Many of the decorative shells were fixed with their cavities upward. In many there was room for a flash drive. But none of them held one.

They had almost given up when Allmen asked, "Carlos! Where would you hide a little flash drive like that?"

Carlos thought about it. He looked around at the cave, looked at the decorations, the fridge, the barbeque, and at the flue. "If it was me, Don John, I would hide something small the way I'd hide something large. Otherwise it would be too easy."

With that he left the grotto.

Allmen followed him. The rain had eased off slightly but was still sufficient to soak both men in seconds.

Carlos walked around the artificial outcrop that held the grotto, looked up, and climbed it nimbly like a staircase. Right at the top the chimney rose from the flue above the grill. Carlos felt around inside, found what he was looking for, pulled, and revealed a large trash bag.

53

There was no one around on the narrow streets of the villa district. The storm had died down, but it was still pouring rain.

Allmen and Carlos walked side by side in silence, heads down, hands deep in their pants pockets.

From far off they saw the brake lights of various vehicles and a crane truck close to Villa Schwarzacker. The storm had blown several heavy boughs down from the old trees, blocking three cars from going forward or backward. City workers in orange rain jackets were busy clearing the obstacles out of the way.

Allmen was worried about his greenhouse under the ancient trees. They stepped up the pace.

But they were in luck. The storm had brought down a few branches, but the gardener's cottage hadn't been hit.

There was another surprise waiting for them, however.

Carlos unlocked the door and let Allmen in first. He entered and switched on the light.

"Small world." It was the voice of Bob, the man from Brookfield Klein. He was sitting on the second step of the stairs to the attic, and blinked in the sudden brightness. He was resting his forearms on his thighs. His right hand was loosely holding a pistol.

"You get wet? I made it before the rain, luckily."

His partner came down the stairs. He nodded to them in silence and stood behind Allmen and Carlos.

"We won't detain you long," Bob said. "You should change into something dry in a minute."

Allmen had composed himself. "What do you want?"

"To make sure you don't have a copy."

"We don't."

"That is what we had assumed. But after you went into Sokolov's house tonight, we thought that might have changed. Has it?"

"You're still sniffing around after us?"

Bob looked at his colleague and said, "Go ahead, Joey."

Joey took a pistol out of his jacket, cocked it, stood in front of Allmen, and kept him covered. Using the other hand, with practiced ease he searched Allmen's pockets and placed their contents on the console under the golden foyer mirror.

He found nothing.

"Before you look in his underpants, search *him*," Bob ordered.

Joey obeyed, and searched Carlos. He found the flash drive in Carlos's right sock.

"Bingo!" Bob grinned. He stood up and walked to the exit. Joey covered his back, then followed him.

"Gringos," Carlos hissed.

54

That same evening, Carlos climbed the steep roof of the gardener's cottage and lifted Sokolov's laptop out of the chimney. He was determined not to give in so quickly.

He tore the new power cord from its plastic case and plugged in the computer.

He wasn't sure what he should search for. "Hedge," "Win," "Brookfield," and "Klein" all drew blanks. He restricted the search to folders and rummaged through them intuitively. He searched programs, but found so many he gave up this tack. Sokolov's hard disk was simply too big. It had a terabyte capacity and was two thirds full. Mostly with data and programs only programmers could understand.

The sound of Allmen playing piano—attempting to calm himself—had long ceased when Carlos had an idea. He narrowed the search according to a timeframe—to the time between the transfer of the data and the arrival of the urgent message from La Route asking him to destroy all traces and hide a backup copy.

The search still produced over nine thousand results.

He narrowed it down further, to folders created during this timeframe.

The search program threw up 234 folders.

One of them was called "Grotto."

"Dios!" Carlos shouted.

It was in the recycle bin. Carlos had to drag it onto the desktop to open it. It held a single file, named "dfdutbce27bg." Carlos opened it and the screen filled with letters and digits that made no sense.

Carlos walked downstairs.

Allmen had already withdrawn to his bedroom. Carlos knocked on the door.

"One moment!" came Allmen's voice. Carlos heard the muffled creaking of the bed and a slight squeak from the wardrobe door, and soon Allmen was standing in front of him in his silk bathrobe.

Carlos apologized for disturbing him so late and led him up the stairs.

Since moving to the gardener's cottage, Allmen had been in Carlos's living room once at most, and had forgotten how tiny it was. Standing up, as there was only one chair, they stared together at the endless series of characters filling the screen as Carlos scrolled down.

"Is that it, the pink diamond?"

"No sé. No idea. But it was in a folder labeled 'Grotto' in the recycle bin. Sokolov had forgotten to empty it."

"Slovenly, as I said."

The parade of characters stopped. The cursor had reached the end of the document.

Allmen and Carlos looked at each other.

"How can we find out if that's what it is?" Allmen's question was to both of them.

"*Saber*. Who knows?" Carlos murmured.

Allmen stood at the attic window and looked out into the night. The storm had risen again and was whipping the twigs of the noble old trees.

He turned from the window and stood back next to Carlos. "I think I know how. But to do that we have to vanish from here."

55

It had stopped raining, but the gusty wind still sent occasional heavy drops pelting from the trees.

In front of the villa stood an old Opel. Its driver got out when he saw them coming, a man of similar stature to Carlos. He was probably a few years older and, like Carlos, had classic Mayan features.

Carlos introduced him as Don Gregorio. They shook hands. *"Mucho gusto,"* they both said.

They drove through the city, continually halted at the barriers set up by the teams clearing the streets of fallen branches, and by fire department vehicles pumping out cellars.

In the outskirts Allmen lost his orientation. Identical apartment buildings from the 1950s and 1960s lined both sides of the poorly lit streets. Industrial buildings alternated with schools, residential complexes, streetcar depots, and forlorn playgrounds. Don Gregorio drove unerringly through the labyrinthine streets before finally stopping outside one of the faceless, five-story blocks. On the tiny balconies were satellite dishes, and from the windows the blue light of televisions flickered.

Don Gregorio led them to the building's entrance, unlocked the door, and went ahead. A range of cooking smells mingled in the hallway. Small dogs yapped from inside the apartments they passed.

On the fourth floor he put Allmen's suitcases down and rang the bell in a particular rhythm.

The door opened immediately. A man, also Central American, opened the door, greeted them wordlessly, and let them in.

The apartment was small. The emulsion painted on the wallpaper had yellowed over the years. It smelled of cigarettes and food.

Don Gregorio led them down the narrow corridor. In the kitchen Allmen saw a few men sitting around a table. They were talking in subdued voices and fell silent as the newcomers passed. In the next room a Spanish-language TV program was playing. Allmen caught a glimpse of a bed four men were using as a sofa.

The next door was closed. A sign saying *"Ocupado"* hung on it. Their host pointed to it. *"El baño,"* he explained. The bathroom.

He opened the door next to it, and they entered a small room. It was furnished with a table and two chairs, a bed, a cupboard, and a bunk bed. On the walls were posters of tourist destinations in Guatemala, El Salvador, and Nicaragua.

Don Gregorio wished them *"Bienvenidos,"* put the suitcases down, and excused himself.

Allmen and Carlos unpacked, then discussed their plan of action. Shortly after midnight they went to sleep.

56

Allmen hadn't shared a bedroom with a man since his time at Charterhouse. And the dorms at Charterhouse were some-what more generous than this room.

Given the spatial restrictions, it was clear from the start they would use the single bed as a sofa. Carlos had given him the choice of top or bottom bunk. Allmen had chosen top, as he envisaged having a more personal space up there. He had no experience of bunk beds.

For Allmen, what was worse than sharing a bedroom with one man was sharing a bathroom and toilet with eight, as it transpired. Over the coming days, this became his biggest motivation for bringing this situation to an end as quickly as possible. Normally a sound sleeper, Allmen had a bad night. He had lain awake till all was still in the apart-ment and he could conduct his evening ablutions in peace and quiet. But even then, for ages he couldn't bring himself to climb down, as he couldn't help imagining what an unfor-tunate sight he would be presenting Carlos, should he still be awake. And once he had finally managed it and lay back up top again, Carlos began to snore. It was less the snoring that kept him awake, more the newly acquired knowledge that his manservant snored.

By the time he fell asleep, the gray light of dawn was seeping through the broken Venetian blinds. When he woke, it was bright, and Carlos's bed was empty.

Allmen waited a while, eventually visited the bathroom, and left it feeling refreshed. A young Nicaraguan was waiting for him with coffee. Don Carlos had asked him to have breakfast ready for Allmen.

It took Allmen a moment to realize there were people who called Carlos "Don Carlos." He thanked the young man, who introduced himself as Gustavo, and followed him into the kitchen. There, sadly now cold, his *huevo ranchero* awaited him—a fried egg with tomato and chili sauce. Gustavo switched on the hotplate, on which two snow-white slices of industrial bread were lying, offered Allmen a chair at the kitchen table, and poured him an Americano—a black drip coffee from the machine. When it started to smell of burned toast, the Nicaraguan turned the slices over.

During breakfast Allmen learned more about his roommates. Don Gregorio was the only legal one. He was the tenant, had official status as an asylum seeker, and a legal job as a cleaner for a supermarket chain.

The others were all immigrants without papers or any pretense of having papers. They were all subtenants of Don Gregorio and paid him or owed him a token rent.

The only task ahead of Allmen this morning was achieved with one phone call to his trusty banking expert Roland Kerbel.

"Do you know anyone high up in the IT department at Brookfield Klein, and could you give me their email address?" he asked on the phone. Kerbel dictated him an address: tbl@brookfield-klein.com.

At eleven Carlos returned. He had been locating Internet cafés far enough away but easily accessible by public transportation. They wanted to send each message from a different address.

He copied the beginning and end of the sequence of letters and digits from the file and pasted it into an email, flagged at the highest level of importance, and addressed to tbl@brookfield-klein.com.

The message was simple: "Contact within 24 hrs, pls."

Beneath the sequence of characters was a link to the site rosadiamant.com, a website Carlos had set up at an Internet café. It displayed the beginning and end of the sequence and the words "To be completed by September 12."

Carlos copied the message onto a flash drive and left the apartment.

The waiting began.

57

During the afternoon Carlos visited two different Internet cafés. Both times in vain. The man from Brookfield Klein had not responded.

Allmen read a book. Then paced back and forth in the tiny room. Then gazed out of the window. The next building was the same as the one he was in. In between the two were twenty yards of concrete slabs with clotheslines stretched above them.

At one point he saw a woman walking around among the laundry. She felt to see which items were still damp, and took the dry ones down, putting them over her arm. A small boy was riding close by on his tricycle. Every so often one of the little wheels got caught in a crevice between slabs. The boy patiently dismounted, made his tricycle roadworthy again, and rode on.

That evening Carlos prepared a Guatemalan dinner for ten. Guacamole, ground beef patties with spicy tomato sauce, fried plantains, black beans, corn tortillas, and chili sauce.

Allmen kept him company.

He watched as Carlos made the avocados into a paste with a fork, mixed them with diced onions, chopped coriander and salt, returning one of the avocado stones to the mixture, then placed his guacamole in the fridge.

"Why do you leave the stone in, Carlos?"

"So the avocado doesn't go black."

"How does that stop it going black?"

"It thinks it's still whole."

Carlos peeled the plantains out of their skins, now almost black.

"The *plátanos* have gone bad, Carlos."

"*Plátanos* are only ripe once their skin is black."

He cut the plantains into thumb-length pieces and placed them on a plate ready to fry.

Allmen bombarded him with further questions. But it didn't help calm his nerves.

Carlos's dinner was a high point in the otherwise monotonous life of the undocumented workers. They forced him to watch the Honduras-El Salvador match from the Central American Cup with them. He sat on the edge of one of the beds in the cramped bedroom/living room and tried to behave like a soccer fan.

Allmen watched politely from the door for a while, then used the excitement surrounding the Honduras go-ahead goal to withdraw to the bathroom and from there to his bedroom. He lay in bed and tried to read by the poor light of the standard lamp, the only light source in the room.

He waited impatiently for Carlos, continually hoping the

cheers and shouts from the TV room signified the end of the game. When Carlos finally slipped quietly into the room, he asked, "What time is it, Carlos?"

"Eleven thirty, Don John."

"Five thirty in New York."

"The Internet cafés will be closed, Don John. We have to wait till tomorrow morning."

Eventually Allmen fell into a restless sleep. When he woke, Carlos's bed was empty.

By the time he'd finished in the bathroom, Carlos was sitting at the table in front of the laptop. He had inserted the little flash drive and opened a document containing the text of an email. It was from tbl@brookfield-klein.com and consisted of just two words and a punctuation character: "Your conditions?"

Allmen and Carlos had already agreed upon the conditions among themselves. Their reply contained simply the international bank account number for Allmen International Inquiries.

And the figure 2.5 million Swiss francs.

58

Allmen knew all too well what it was like to have no money. Nevertheless he had always lived as if he had lots. Being forced to live as if he had none, and all that while waiting for millions, was a new experience for him.

The men he was living with had no money at all and lived that way too. They had nothing else either. No papers, no work, no future.

He would have loved to give them a few tips on how to cheat the world, and yourself, into thinking you have money. But he soon realized these people couldn't act as if they had money. They didn't know what it was like to have any.

Allmen decided that as soon as the millions had come in, he must give his roommates some money. To practice with.

Twice he succumbed to cabin fever and left the apartment, without informing Carlos. The first time he went to a nearby Indian restaurant, which looked elegant from the outside but shabby on the inside. He ordered a tasting menu. All the curries had the same flavor, all cooked a long time in advance and quickly reheated. Yet he still enjoyed the change of scenery and the feeling of being a real person.

The second time he ended up in a local tearoom. Apart from him there were just waitresses in training and elderly women. He ordered a latte and a croissant and missed his Café Viennois.

Carlos made no comment when Allmen returned from his outings. But he let his *patrón* sense what he thought about this lack of discipline.

The days in the overcrowded apartment were long. And the way they both stared at the laptop, like a kettle that refused to boil, made them longer.

At one point Carlos asked, "How can they be sure we won't keep a copy?"

"They can't be sure. But they'll have to take the risk."

"Por qué?" Why?

"It's the safest bet."

"Ojalá." Let's hope so.

On the third day, the penultimate day before the deadline, an email arrived. "Procedure?" it asked. And "Guarantees?"

They replied, "Procedure: delivery of the flash drive via DHL on receipt of the bank transfer. Guarantees: word of honor from Johann Friedrich von Allmen."

On the final day of the deadline Carlos travelled continually between the apartment and the Internet cafés, logging into the Allmen International bank account on an almost hourly basis.

When the deadline came, the money still hadn't appeared.

"Now what?" Allmen asked.

Without hesitating for a second, Carlos copied another

large section from the beginning and end of the file onto the website.

Carlos returned from the next monitoring trip with a message from Brookfield Klein. "Stop. Transfer in progress."

Neither Allmen nor Carlos slept much that night. But they were still wide awake when they checked the Allmen International account next day. It showed a balance of 2,503,114.35 Swiss francs.

Allmen sounded almost offended: "I didn't realize we still had over three thousand in the account."

59

In the excitement Allmen transferred a hundred thousand Swiss francs to Don Gregorio. Twenty as capital for his venture, plus ten thousand for everyone in the apartment so they could get some practice at having money.

"They'll send the money home, Don John," Carlos warned him.

Allmen reflected, then said, "Even that will give them a sense of what it's like to have money."

They all gathered in the windows to watch the departure of Don John and Carlos in Herr Arnold's 1978 Cadillac Fleetwood. They watched as the window on Allmen's side was lowered and a slender hand with white cuffs waved to them. Then the three men vanished into their other world.

Epilogue

Once Carlos's share had been deducted, all outstanding debts settled, and the overdrafts on both his personal bank accounts paid off, Allmen was left with a credit of just over nine hundred thousand francs.

He put part of it into his ongoing expenditure—expanding his wardrobe, acquiring certain items for his art deco collection, sorely depleted over the past two years—and on two weeks of Indian summer in the Terrace Suite at the Wheatleigh Hotel in Lenox, Massachusetts. Very finely refurbished indeed.

But perhaps due to his recent exposure to genuine poverty he put the lion's share into a portfolio of stocks compiled with the help of his old friend, the banker Roland Kerbel. It still came to over half a million.

His butler and business partner Carlos continued to work as a part-time janitor and gardener for K, C, L & D, although given his financial situation he was no longer dependent on this pocket change. But it was a welcome contribution to the salary of Maria Moreno, who was now assured a permanent position. Allmen loved staff, and Carlos loved Maria Moreno.

Carlos had placed part of his capital in a savings account, but the majority hung, wrapped in watertight, fireproof packaging, halfway up the chimney of the gardener's cottage.

And so it withstood the sudden crash that came shortly before Christmas, in which Allmen's portfolio, poorly chosen by Roland Kerbel, lost over half its value.

There was much speculation in the media as to what had triggered the crash. The culprit was believed to be an unidentified high-frequency trading program.

My brother, Dr. Daniel Suter-Châtelanat, enlightened me on the subject of high-frequency trading. The programmer and IT expert Ivan Melnychuk gave me tips on how it's possible to lose a lot of money in a short span of time on the stock market. My editor, Ursula Baumhauer, and my wife, Margrith Nay Suter, supported me as ever with very constructive criticism, and my little daughter, Ana, accidently deleted a passage on the screen, which in hindsight proved to be superfluous. My heartfelt thanks to all of you.

—Martin Suter

ALLMEN AND THE DRAGONFLIES
BY MARTIN SUTER

This is the first of a series of humorous detective novels devoted to a memorable gentleman thief who, with his Guatemalan butler Carlos, creates an investigative firm to recover missing precious objects. Johann Friedrich von Allmen, a bon vivant of dandified refinement, has exhausted his family fortune by living in Old World grandeur despite present-day financial constraints. Forced to downscale, Allmen inhabits the garden house of his former Zurich estate. Pressured to pay off mounting debts, he absconds with priceless Art Nouveau bowls decorated with a dragonfly motif and embarks on a high-risk, potentially violent bid to cash them in.

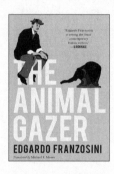

THE ANIMAL GAZER
BY EDGARDO FRANZOSINI

A hypnotic novel inspired by the strange and fascinating life of sculptor Rembrandt Bugatti, brother of the fabled automaker. With World War I closing in and the Belle Epoque teetering to a close, Bugatti is increasingly obsessed with zoo animals. He closely observes the caged baboons, giraffes and panthers, finding empathy with their plight. Edgardo Franzosini recreates the young artist's life with intense lyricism, passion, and sensitivity.

THE MADELEINE PROJECT
BY CLARA BEAUDOUX

A young woman moves into a Paris apartment and discovers a storage room filled with the belongings of the previous owner, a certain Madeleine who died in her late nineties, and whose treasured possessions nobody seems to want. In an audacious act of journalism driven by personal curiosity and humane tenderness, Clara Beaudoux embarks on *The Madeleine Project*, documenting what she finds on Twitter with text and photographs, introducing the world to an unsung 20th century figure.

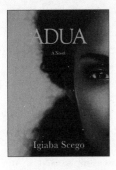

ADUA
BY IGIABA SCEGO

Adua, an immigrant from Somalia to Italy, has lived in Rome for nearly forty years. She came seeking freedom from a strict father and an oppressive regime, but her dreams of film stardom ended in shame. Now that the civil war in Somalia is over, her homeland calls her. She must decide whether to return and reclaim her inheritance, but also how to take charge of her own story and build a future.

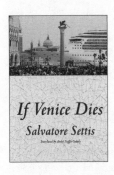

IF VENICE DIES
BY SALVATORE SETTIS

Internationally renowned art historian Salvatore Settis ignites a new debate about the Pearl of the Adriatic and cultural patrimony at large. In this fiery blend of history and cultural analysis, Settis argues that "hit-and-run" visitors are turning Venice and other landmark urban settings into shopping malls and theme parks. This is a passionate plea to secure the soul of Venice, written with consummate authority, wide-ranging erudition and élan.

A VERY RUSSIAN CHRISTMAS

This is Russian Christmas celebrated in supreme pleasure and pain by the greatest of writers, from Dostoevsky and Tolstoy to Chekhov and Teffi. The dozen stories in this collection will satisfy every reader, and with their wit, humor, and tenderness, packed full of sentimental songs, footmen, whirling winds, solitary nights, snow drifts, and hopeful children, the collection proves that Nobody Does Christmas Like the Russians.

OBLIVION
BY SERGEI LEBEDEV

In one of the first 21st century Russian novels to probe the legacy of the Soviet prison camp system, a young man travels to the vast wastelands of the Far North to uncover the truth about a shadowy neighbor who saved his life, and whom he knows only as Grandfather II. Emerging from today's Russia, where the ills of the past are being forcefully erased from public memory, this masterful novel represents an epic literary attempt to rescue history from the brink of oblivion.

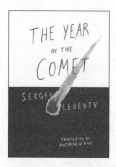

THE YEAR OF THE COMET
BY SERGEI LEBEDEV

A story of a Russian boyhood and coming of age as the Soviet Union is on the brink of collapse. Lebedev depicts a vast empire coming apart at the seams, transforming a very public moment into something tender and personal, and writes with stunning beauty and shattering insight about childhood and the growing consciousness of a boy in the world.

MOVING THE PALACE
BY CHARIF MAJDALANI

A young Lebanese adventurer explores the wilds of Africa, encountering an eccentric English colonel in Sudan and enlisting in his service. In this lush chronicle of far-flung adventure, the military recruit crosses paths with a compatriot who has dismantled a sumptuous palace and is transporting it across the continent on a camel caravan. This is a captivating modern-day Odyssey in the tradition of Bruce Chatwin and Paul Theroux.

THE 6:41 TO PARIS
BY JEAN-PHILIPPE BLONDEL

Cécile, a stylish 47-year-old, has spent the weekend visiting her parents outside Paris. By Monday morning, she's exhausted. These trips back home are stressful and she settles into a train compartment with an empty seat beside her. But it's soon occupied by a man she recognizes as Philippe Leduc, with whom she had a passionate affair that ended in her brutal humiliation 30 years ago. In the fraught hour and a half that ensues, Cécile and Philippe hurtle towards the French capital in a psychological thriller about the pain and promise of past romance.

ON THE RUN WITH MARY
BY JONATHAN BARROW

Shining moments of tender beauty punctuate this story of a youth on the run after escaping from an elite English boarding school. At London's Euston Station, the narrator meets a talking dachshund named Mary and together they're off on escapades through posh Mayfair streets and jaunts in a Rolls-Royce. But the youth soon realizes that the seemingly sweet dog is a handful; an alcoholic, nymphomaniac, drug-addicted mess who can't stay out of pubs or off the dance floor. *On the Run with Mary* mirrors the horrors and the joys of the terrible 20th century.

THE MADONNA OF NOTRE DAME
BY ALEXIS RAGOUGNEAU

Fifty thousand people jam into Notre Dame Cathedral to celebrate the Feast of the Assumption. The next morning, a beautiful young woman clothed in white kneels at prayer in a cathedral side chapel. But when someone accidentally bumps against her, her body collapses. She has been murdered. This thrilling novel illuminates shadowy corners of the world's most famous cathedral, shedding light on good and evil with suspense, compassion and wry humor.

THE LAST WEYNFELDT
BY MARTIN SUTER

Adrian Weynfeldt is an art expert in an international auction house, a bachelor in his mid-fifties living in a grand Zurich apartment filled with costly paintings and antiques. Always correct and well-mannered, he's given up on love until one night—entirely out of character for him—Weynfeldt decides to take home a ravishing but unaccountable young woman and gets embroiled in an art forgery scheme that threatens his buttoned up existence. This refined page-turner moves behind elegant bourgeois facades into darker recesses of the heart.

THE LAST SUPPER
BY KLAUS WIVEL

Alarmed by the oppression of 7.5 million Christians in the Middle East, journalist Klaus Wivel traveled to Iraq, Lebanon, Egypt, and the Palestinian territories to learn about their fate. He found a minority under threat of death and humiliation, desperate in the face of rising Islamic extremism and without hope their situation will improve. An unsettling account of a severely beleaguered religious group living, so it seems, on borrowed time. Wivel asks, Why have we not done more to protect these people?

New Vessel Press

To purchase these books and for a full listing of New Vessel Press titles, visit our website at www.newvesselpress.com

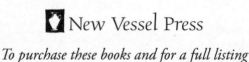